A Mug's

by

Andrew Hawthorne

Edited by Christopher Watt

Prologue

In March 2020, the United Kingdom was in a state of blind panic as the COVID 19 pandemic started to spread quickly through the population resulting in a high number of deaths. The virus, which preyed upon the weak and infirm in society, was particularly damaging to the elderly population who had little or no protection from this highly infectious bug. The Government had to act quickly and ordered a complete lockdown of the country to stop the spread of COVID but it was too little too late.

On 14th May 2020, the UK Government published its plans for a national furlough scheme in response to the lockdown that it had imposed on its citizens and businesses alike. That was the first time I had ever heard the word 'furlough' used in that context and little did I know then, it would change my life forever.

I was working as a supervisor in the local leisure centre in Dumbarton before the lockdown came into force. At first, I was sent home by my boss on full pay and about three weeks later he called me to say that we had been furloughed until further notice. I know what you are thinking - how can being furloughed change your life forever? Get a grip Billy! After all, you just sit at home, get paid eighty percent of your wages and wait until the lockdown ends and then go back to work. Easy, yes, but no one mentions the boredom and low self-esteem associated with being on furlough and it's not as if you can make good use of that time as there's absolutely nothing to do during the lockdown. Everywhere, with the exception of grocery stores and supermarkets, is closed; there are no pubs, no cinemas, no restaurants, nothing! So, what does a man do with himself to keep himself amused? Answer – watch the telly. Well, I did that, for a while, and then I read some books that I had been meaning to read for ages. This helped pass the time for a while but eventually the boredom set in. Yes, I kept myself fit by exercising at home, just like that bloke with the long hair and beard on the telly, but that was not enough. I had worked all my life since the age of sixteen and had never considered how mind-blowingly boring life would be without having work to do. "Surely you helped out around the house?" I hear you ask. "Surely you did some housework, fixed things you had promised to fix but never got round to, etc., etc., etc." Well yes, I did all these things and the first few months were okay but after a while I ran out of things to fix or materials to fix things with. I was bored. Completely and utterly bored out of my mind. So much so, that doing the ironing and hoovering were the high points until one day I decided to download a betting app on my phone. I remember it clearly; it was just after the decision had been made to allow football to return behind closed doors. Sky was already showing games in the Bundesliga as British football had not restarted and so there I was, sitting in my living room, watching the telly when the Sky Bet advert came on for the one-hundredth time and so I decided to download the app for a bit of fun.

Yes, I know! What a fool, what a loser, gambling is for mugs, bookies never lose, yadda, yadda, yadda! Well, you would be right and I did lose, and do you know what, I didn't even mind losing. The buzz of the occasional win kept me going. It was all just a bit of fun. A few pounds here, a few pounds there. After all, I didn't want my wife Maureen to find out that I was gambling. She would not approve! Therefore, I kept the stakes small and consequently my losses and my occasional wins were small.

At first, I just went with my gut feeling when trying to predict the results and failed miserably when betting on the Bundesliga; I knew nothing about German football other than that Bayern Munich and Borussia Dortmund were good. These were teams that I recognised from the Champions League. So, I started picking British football teams after the league games restarted. I recognised and picked those teams that I thought I knew reasonably well. There was the occasional game which you might describe as being a banker but they were few and far between and it was soon very obvious that I knew a lot less about football than I thought I did and so my losses, as small as they were, began to build up. I used an old bank account to deposit my stakes as this was the easiest way to hide my losses, but I knew that after a while Maureen would notice the small transfers from the joint account to my personal account and start to become suspicious. I even had an excuse ready if she asked – I was saving up for her 40th birthday to get her a special surprise. I know - I'm a bad person, not just a secret gambler but a liar too. I should have stopped right there, right at that moment when I created the lie to cover up my secret vice. I did try but it was like an addiction. No strike that - *it was an addiction*. I could not stop myself and as I knew I had to do something to reduce the losses that's when I decided to take my gambling habit to another level. I started to study the form but perhaps more importantly I studied my losses and learned from my mistakes. One benefit of using the gambling app is that it saves your gambling history which means you can see all your losses and wins and analyse them, which was just what I did.

I had no idea where this new strategy would lead and if I had the chance to go back in time, give myself an almighty slap in the face, and stop, just stop gambling, that would have been the time to do it. But I didn't!

Chapter One

The Burgh Bar was a long-established public house located in the heart of Dumbarton's High Street. It was extremely popular in the eighties but recently was struggling to contend with the surge of newer, larger public houses that had moved into the High Street and were attracting most of the youngsters. This meant that traditional pubs like the Burgh Bar relied even more heavily on their regulars to survive and even the regulars were becoming an ever-decreasing group. On top of that, the COVID-19 lockdown had hit the small pubs hard and only a few had managed to reopen their doors.

Thankfully, the Burgh Bar was one of them; otherwise, Billy Taylor and his mates would have needed to find a new drinking hole.

Billy had agreed to meet his two old school pals, Eddie O'Neill and Martin Toal in their favourite pub on the first day it reopened after lockdown.

As Billy walked towards the pub, he could feel a sense of excitement and nervousness - not only because he had not seen his pals face to face for such a long time but because he had something exciting that he wanted to share with them.

As he made his way along the beleaguered High Street, he could see the damage that the lockdown had done to some of the smaller shops; many of them had closed completely while others had reduced hours due to a lack of staff and were advertising for replacements on their windows. However, it was no surprise to Billy that the betting shops, affectionately known as 'the bookies' had also reopened. Billy wondered how wee Willie Rennie, the owner of the Burgh Bar, had managed to keep it afloat without any custom all this time. Presumably, the government had suspended the rates or done something to help small businesses. He had heard that some businesses were eligible to claim grants from the Council but even then, many were struggling to keep going with most staff put on furlough or made redundant.

When he reached the entrance to the pub Billy stopped for a moment, took a deep breath and released it slowly. He put on his facemask, pulled the door open and immediately he could smell the sour aroma of the beer drifting gently towards him, being pulled by the draught that the open door had created.

Billy looked around the pub and immediately noticed that it was different; there were very few tables and chairs laid out compared to normal and some of the side booths had Perspex panels separating the spaces, but most unusual of all was the absence of any punters standing at the bar. He then saw the sign "Table Service Only" and nodded to himself. *Well, this is different.*

Eddie and Martin had arrived before Billy and had taken up a table in the middle of the room. "Over here Billy," Eddie shouted, and waved his hands in the air to get the attention of his pal.

Billy smiled and marched over to the small table where Eddie and Martin were sitting waiting. Eddie looked as wiry and as strong as ever while Martin looked even fatter than before - a walking heart attack. Well perhaps that's not very accurate… Martin never walked anywhere if he could help it.

Billy removed his mask and put out his hand, offering to shake and was promptly offered a set of knuckles instead. "Of course, what am I thinking? No shaking hands, right? Well, I suppose the knuckle rub is better than the elbow rub," said Billy. "Have you seen the bold Boris on the telly, dancing around trying to rub elbows in his ill-fitting suit? Weird right? Anyway, how are you both, it's been too long?"

"Aye, no' bad Billy," said Eddie.

"Me too," said Martin less convincingly.

Billy looked down at the table that had two half-filled glasses of lager sitting waiting to be finished.

"Can I get you guys a drink? I see you've started already."

"Ach go on then," said Martin who was quick to accept the offer, promptly picking up his glass and taking a large gulp of the amber liquid.

"Same again?" Billy asked.

"Aye," said Eddie. "But you'll need to call that wee lassie over to order them; it's table service only."

Billy nodded, sat down and signalled to the young woman who was standing behind the bar. "Can we have three pints of Tennent's lager, please?" he shouted across the room. His raised voice drew the attention of a couple of rough looking customers who were sitting a few tables away. The two men scowled at Billy for disturbing their peace and then went back to sipping their pints.

The girl nodded, went for some glasses and started drawing the pints. Within minutes she brought the drinks over to the table. "Do you want to start a tab or pay as you go?" she asked.

Billy looked at his two pals who both shrugged their shoulders as if to say *it's up to you,* and then he made a quick decision. "Pay as you go, please. What do I owe you for this round?"

"That'll be £12.60 thanks," she said. "Oh, and it's card only I'm afraid."

Billy took out his wallet and found his debit card. The young bartender came back over and Billy touched the contactless card against the small screen which was followed by the sound of a bleep confirming that the payment had gone through the system.

"This is all very weird isn't," said Billy looking around the pub. "Table service, card payment only... but still, it's good to be getting back to some form of normal again, isn't it?"

"You can say that again," said Eddie. "Thank God the building trade was one of the first to return to work, well outdoors anyway. I'd have cut my wrists if I had to stay at home for any longer."

"Are you back yet, Martin?" asked Billy.

"Aye, but not for long the way things are going."

"What do you mean? They're not going to close your branch, are they? I thought the banks, of all places, would be safe," said Billy.

"Yeah, and so did I, but there's just been an announcement that they're going to shut sixty branches across the country and my boss thinks it's just a matter of time before it's our turn."

Billy shook his head in disbelief. "I'm sorry to hear that mate."

Martin suddenly perked up. "Aye well, let's no' dwell on it and try and enjoy ourselves. What's that saying, 'Live for the day!' or something like that? You know... the Latin thingy-ma-jig."

Eddie turned towards Billy. "Did you no' study Latin at school Billy?"

"Aye, and a lot of good it did me - working for the Council, well the Leisure Trust, but yes, I took Latin in second year." Billy thought back to a wasted year studying what he considered to be one of the most boring subjects on the planet and smiled to himself.

"Bloody teacher talked my mother into it. Thought I was going to be a doctor or a lawyer or something… nae chance."

"Aye, I think that teacher fancied you and that's why she wanted you in her class," said Eddie winking at Martin.

"Don't be daft," said Billy, but then he thought that maybe Eddie had a point. Billy had been a good-looking boy back then; he was tall for his age and looked older than most of his pals, so perhaps Eddie was right.

"So, *genius*, what is Latin for 'live for the day'," asked Eddie.

"It's not 'live for the day' it's 'seize the day' but I suppose it means the same thing. The Latin is *carpe diem.*"

"That's it. Seize the day! That's what I meant to say," said Martin, who then took a large gulp of his lager and was feeling very pleased with himself.

"Do you know something, Billy," said Eddie. "I've always thought that you were far too clever to be stuck in that leisure centre. I can remember when you were top of the class for maths. You got a prize or something, didn't you?"

Billy nodded modestly. "Yes, that was in fourth year, just before I left school. So what? I'm happy working in the leisure centre. I enjoy it. How many people can say that about their work?"

Eddie and Martin both nodded in agreement and took another swig of their beers. Billy suddenly remembered what it was he wanted to share with his pals.

"Hey, have you two ever tried those gambling apps, you know, the ones you can download onto your phone?"

Eddie was the first to respond. "Yes, and I lost a bloody fortune so I got rid of the bloody thing. Far too convenient and far too tempting if you ask me. Don't tell me you're into gambling now. It's a mug game Billy, surely you of all people must know that the bookies never lose."

Billy sat there grinning as his mates waxed lyrical about the money that they had lost over the years and then decided it was time to let them into his little secret. He took his phone out of his pocket, opened his betting app and called up his balance - his very healthy balance.

"Have a look at this," he said as he passed his phone over to Eddie, who was sitting on his left.

"So what? They are all the same, they... fucking hell Billy. You've got over a thousand quid on here." Eddie stared at the small screen in disbelief and then passed it over to Martin to double-check.

"Fuck me," said Martin. How on earth did you accumulate that lot?"

Billy shuffled his seat closer to the table and both his pals did the same, sensing he was about to reveal the secret of the century. "I think I know how to beat the bookies."

Chapter Two

DC Jim Armstrong and DC Paul Black, Dumbarton CID, were sitting in the front seats of an unmarked car watching the rear entrance to the Rock Taxis building. Their task, which had been given to them by DI Redding, was quite simple - watch whoever comes and goes and, if possible, get a photograph but be discreet and do not get spotted, under any circumstances.

The Dumbarton CID had received an anonymous tip-off that Kevin McGrath, a well-known local hoodlum, and owner of Rock Taxis had started to deal in drugs and, allegedly, was using his taxis to deliver the goods to customers all over the Dumbarton area. In addition to the tip-off, the local police had noticed an increase in the availability of drugs in the area and already had strong suspicions about McGrath. What they didn't have was any hard evidence, certainly not enough to get a warrant for a search of the premises or his home.

DI Redding wanted to know who was doing business with McGrath and where he was getting his supply. It was not enough to put McGrath behind bars, she wanted his supplier! She had been involved in a major drug bust before transferring to Dumbarton and knew from experience that there must be a bigger shark swimming around somewhere out there who was supplying McGrath with drugs to distribute in *her* area. She was desperate to bring down the whole network, but she knew that level of investigation would need to involve working with the Regional Organised Crime at some point, which was fine by her providing she had enough evidence.

With exception of the occasional toilet break, the two detectives had been in the car for just over six hours, and nothing had happened. No one other than the two taxi-staff had entered the building since their surveillance had started at 8 a.m. Consequently, the two detectives were beginning to get tired and bored with the job when *finally,* McGrath turned up in his wee black Audi TT. The two police officers could only dream of owning such a car.

McGrath got out of his car and immediately made a call on his mobile phone before walking slowly towards his office.

DC Armstrong took out his notebook and recorded the time that McGrath entered the building, 14:13.

"Now let's see who else turns up today," he said, relieved that there was now some chance of activity worth reporting.

Chapter Three

Peter Macdonald stood nervously waiting for his fiancée, Claire Redding, to arrive. He checked his watch for the fifth time within the last minute and then straightened his tie and adjusted the suit jacket that he had picked up from Slater's especially for the occasion. He had been looking forward to this day for such a long time; he and Claire had hoped to tie the knot quickly after their engagement, but the lockdown had put an end to that plan. And so, they had been patient and waited for the restrictions to be relaxed before setting a date with the local registrar.

The Marriage Room was located on the first floor of the Municipal Buildings, Dumbarton. The former Council Chamber had recently been redecorated and was beautifully lit with the large bay window to the front and intricate stained-glass windows to the rear. It was a stunning room - however, the virus was still out there, and accordingly social distancing and facemasks were still mandatory for all guests, even at weddings. The maximum capacity for the room was restricted to only twenty persons due to the two-metre rule but that had not put off Peter and Claire, who had only wanted a few guests to witness their big day.

Claire's mum and a few of her other close relatives were present and were sitting on one side of the room. On the opposite side of the small aisle, DS Brian O'Neill and his wife Agnes, both of whom had agreed to be witnesses to the marriage, were sitting in the front row. A few of Peter's closest work colleagues were sitting behind Brian and Agnes. Peter did not have any family that he knew of; his mum had died of a drug overdose when he was a teenager and his father had disappeared before he was born. His loyal dog, Sally, had been left with a neighbour, as she could not be trusted to behave herself at such an occasion. Claire had made it clear that she was very happy for Sally to be there, but Peter did not want the additional stress of trying to control Sally during the ceremony.

Peter heard the large door of the Chamber open and turned towards the guests who were sitting behind him. It was very surreal seeing everyone wearing facemasks, but it was unavoidable and most of the guests had managed to match their masks to their outfits. The bride and groom, however, were allowed to remove their masks during the ceremony but that was as far as the rules allowed.

The young female registrar entered the room, made her way to the front and stood behind the small desk that had been dressed in white linen and had a large bouquet of white roses as a centrepiece. Once in position, she removed her mask and addressed the room. "Ladies and Gentlemen, please be upstanding for the bride." She turned and switched on the small CD player in the corner of the room. The Chamber soon filled with the sound of Mendelssohn's Wedding March. Peter's heart jumped and his stomach churned as Claire entered the room accompanied by her father. She was the most beautiful thing he had ever seen and the plain white dress, which she had chosen to wear, highlighted her stunning figure more than any traditional wedding dress ever could. He was the luckiest man on the planet and every inch of his being felt that to be the indisputable truth; he was absolutely beaming with joy but most of all his heart was bursting full of his love for Claire.

As she stood beside him, he turned towards her and lifted the short white veil that had covered her face. She smiled up at Peter who leaned down and kissed her cheek as gently as he had ever kissed her. Her perfume filled his head with wonderful memories of their short life together and although it had not been very easy at first, he was delighted that they had now reached a point where both were in absolute harmony with each other's inner desires.

The registrar gave the couple a moment to compose themselves and then turned off the music before commencing the ceremony. In the pre-wedding meeting, the registrar had told them that the wedding could be as long or as short as they wanted. They could also have as many songs or readings as they wanted. In the end, they had decided to keep it short and simple and so the ceremony was all over before they knew it. The registrar announced them to be man and wife and Peter took the opportunity to kiss his 'wife' in public for the first time.

There were tears everywhere, Claire's mum, of course. Even Brian could be seen wiping his eyes, pretending he had a rogue eye lash or something similar. After signing the marriage schedule and having some photographs taken inside the Chamber, they all went outdoors to the fresh air to get a few more photos in the grounds of the handsome red sandstone building. They stood underneath the old archway which stood proudly on the far side of the building, facing the library. The Municipal Building had been gifted to the people of Dumbarton and was maintained by the Council on behalf of its citizens as part of the Common Good. It had been refurbished to a very high standard; the exterior stonework had taken approximately two years to repair but it had been well worth the wait. As they stood there posing for photographs, Peter and Claire could not be happier.

Chapter Four

"Go on then Billy, tell us how you did it?" asked Eddie, eager to discover the secret.

Billy proceeded to take a bit of paper out of his pocket. "I thought you might ask so I wrote it down as best I could, but I'll need to explain a few things as I go as it's not as simple as you might think." He looked around the room again to check that no one was listening in to their conversation. "Right, here goes. First things first. Choose football or another sport where the outcome is predictable. What I mean by that is that you should choose a sport where the bookmakers can predict the result with some level of accuracy – let them do the research, do not rely on your own instincts. The whole system is based on reducing the risk of losing."

Martin was the first to interrupt. "Hold on a minute Billy. Are you saying we shouldn't try to win? That doesn't make any sense." He looked at Eddie for support and could see that his pal was also struggling to follow what Billy was getting at.

"What I mean is… by reducing the risk of losing you increase the chance of winning but you can't get greedy and take big risks. But let's not get caught up in that bit for now. Here are some basic rules that you need to follow to reduce the risk of losing. One: never bet on horse racing or greyhound racing as the risk is too high. Two: when betting on football, look for home teams to win with the lowest odds and check their form. If they lost or drew their last game, ditch them. You are looking for low odds like 4/11, 2/9, and so on. Remember, the bookies have done their homework so all you are doing is following the games where they think the result is certain or as close to certain as you can get. Three: do not focus on one league or even one country. Look for the lowest odds across all the leagues – the app makes that easy. Four: never bet on cup competitions unless the result is an absolute stick on. You know like Celtic versus Albion Rovers or Rangers versus Dumbarton."

"Hold on a minute, Dumbarton are no' that bad," said Eddie, smiling.

Billy was quick to respond. "Well in that case don't bet on them. Five: only select five or six games at a time and only use multiplier bets like a Heinz or Lucky 63. As I said before, do not be greedy and try to win big the first time as there will always be some days when you may make a loss, so keep your losses as small as possible. Right, where was I? Oh aye, six: only bet a small amount on each of your bets, for example 5p or 10p so the cost of your stake is not too high! Aim for a maximum spend of five or six quid per bet; the trick is to accumulate a fund over a long period. Seven: do not be tempted to recoup any losses by gambling again on the same day. Eight: only bet what you can afford to lose. Always be canny, as nothing is guaranteed. However, rule number nine is the most important rule of all and this one, for me, is the game changer: you must keep your eye on your bets during the play and if at any point you see that you have been offered a cash-out equal to double your stake, take the money. Don't get greedy!" Billy sat back and looked at his two pals who seemed completely underwhelmed by the information he had just shared with them.

"Is that it?" asked Eddie.

"What do you mean, is that it?" replied Billy feeling a little deflated by the response. "I've just told you how to beat the bookies and you're sitting there like… like… I don't know… like you've lost a winning lottery ticket."

"It's just that it all seems so simple, too simple if you know what I mean," said Martin.

Billy nodded. "It does, but the whole thing also depends on discipline." He could see his pals were still sceptical. He looked at his watch and then made a quick decision. "Okay, here's what we are going to do. I've already selected six games today and have put on a 'Lucky 63' multiplier at ten pence per bet so a total stake of £6.30. I'll give you both the same six teams to bet on. Now, you go across to the bookies and put the same bet on as me and

I'll show you how it works. You'll need to be quick though, the first game starts at three o'clock."

Eddie looked at Martin and they nodded. "You're on. You get the next round in and we'll be back in a few minutes," said Martin.

Billy did as he was asked and then sat waiting for his two pals to come back. He took out his telephone and opened the app and immediately clicked on the 'my bets' button to see the games that he had selected. He could see that if he had predicted all six results correctly, the total winnings would be £27.84. However, he would only try to win it all if he was confident that all six games were guaranteed; this was the crux of his process. He knew that there would come a point in time when he would need to decide to take either his winnings or let the bet run to the end. It was all about nerve, discipline and judgement and he was not confident that his pals had any of those qualities. That said, he was excited at the prospect of another betting challenge. It was indeed Billy versus the bookies and so far, he was winning!

Chapter Five

After the photographer was completely satisfied that he had taken all the photographs specified by the couple, not to mention a few others inspired by their beautiful surroundings, he said his farewells and made his way to the reception venue to capture the couple arriving in the wedding car.

Claire had wanted a small wedding and that's exactly what she got, but Peter was determined to make the most of the day and had booked a small room in the nearby Cameron House Hotel for the wedding meal, cake, etc. According to Peter, the five-star hotel, which had only just reopened following a major fire, had been beautifully refurbished and was the perfect location for their reception.

The happy couple waved to their family and friends from their luxurious car, a classic 1971 Rolls Royce Silver Shadow. They headed off to the hotel still buzzing from the excitement of the occasion and a little relieved to have the ceremonial part out of the way.

"This car is gorgeous, Peter. I hope you didn't spend a fortune on it."

Peter turned towards Claire and smiled. "Never you mind how much it costs, Claire Redding - eh I mean... Claire Macdonald. This is our day so just enjoy it."

"Oh, that sounds weird doesn't it, *Claire Macdonald*," she said. "I don't think I'm ever going to get used to it." Claire paused momentarily. "Are you still okay with me using *Redding* at work? Haven't changed your mind now that we're married?"

"Claire, I honestly couldn't care any less about what you call yourself at work. All I care about is that we are married and will be together for the rest of our lives." He moved nearer to Claire and kissed her on the cheek.

The driver of the vehicle looked at the couple through the rear mirror and smiled. He had made this journey many times with many different couples but there was something about this pair that he liked, something that felt right about them. "Do you want to go direct to the hotel or would you like me to take you further down the loch and then turn back. It will give your guests more time to arrive at the hotel and means they will be there to greet you as you arrive," he explained.

"That's a great idea," said Peter.

Claire nodded in agreement. "Maybe just as far as Luss and back. We wouldn't want to keep our guests waiting too long and..." She was interrupted by the sound of a mobile phone. The noise was coming from the small white purse which was sitting on her lap. Peter stared at Claire accusingly. "You brought your phone to our wedding?"

"Sorry, I thought I had put it on silent. It was just in case of emergencies. I'm sure it's nothing. I have a team on stakeout and…"

"Claire. Stop! Just give me the phone and we'll forget all about it." Peter put out his hand to receive the phone.

Claire knew there was no point arguing. She had promised Peter that she would leave her work behind her today and now that she had been caught, she had no choice. She took the phone out of the bag, turned it off and handed it over to Peter who slipped it into his jacket pocket beside his speech.

The car turned at Luss and headed back to the hotel where, as the driver had predicted, their guests and the photographer were eagerly awaiting their arrival. The driver got out of the car and opened the passenger door at Claire's side to allow her to exit gracefully to the applause of their guests who had gathered round the car. They felt like royalty.

Chapter Six

Eddie and Martin returned from the bookies full of excitement and could not wait for the first match to kick off. At 3 p.m., Billy took out his phone and opened the betting app. Immediately, all six of the games he had selected were showing red.

"Okay, I'll check the results every ten minutes to see what happens and then I'll talk you through the process."

After ten minutes, Billy looked at the app again and showed it to his pals. "Look, two of our teams have turned green already and it's offering a cash-out value at £3.60. What we want to happen is the results in other games to go green early as that will force the cash out payment to rise and if it goes high enough before the games end then I will accept the cash-out on offer," Billy explained.

"What if they are all green?" asked Martin.

"Ah well, that's when I will have a real decision to make. Do I cash out early and take the guaranteed payment or do I risk taking less in the hope that all results stay the same?"

"I suppose it depends on the scores," offered Eddie.

Billy nodded. "Exactly, if all teams are sitting on a good lead by two or three clear goals then the risk of losing is low but if even one of those teams is only one up that's when it gets interesting. Now, remember, this system is designed to prevent loss and make gains over the long term. I have learned the hard way not to get greedy."

"I think I get it now," said Martin.

Billy smiled. "Okay, let's get some more drinks in and have another look at the scores in ten minutes or so."

After another ten minutes had passed, Billy opened his app again and could see that four of the games were showing green but one of the other two games was showing that the away side were winning one nil. "Oh crap, that's not good," said Billy.

"What do you mean?" asked Eddie. "We have four wins showing at the moment!"

"Yes, but the cash out value will remain low if that result stays the same. The bookies will only offer you a higher cash out value if they think they have a chance of losing more. Remember, this is a multiplier bet so to lose one game has a significant impact on the total amount of winnings."

Billy looked at both of his pals who were nodding slowly but he could tell from the glazed expression in their eyes that neither really understood what he was getting at. "Anyway, it's too early to worry yet. Anything can happen in football!"

"Aye it's a game of two halves!" said Martin, mimicking the nasal tones of Chick Young, a well-known Scottish football commentator.

"Oh, don't you start!" said Eddie jokingly and pushed Martin, who overreacted and feigned falling off his chair.

"Hoy, ref, did you see that? Get the card oot!" shouted Martin, who was now clearly feeling the benefit of the beers.

"You two behave or we'll get chucked out of here," said Billy, with a wry smile on his face.

"Ach, let them try," said Eddie who was always ready for a scrap after a few beers.

"Whose turn is it to get the beers in?" asked Billy, quickly changing the subject.

"Martin, you're het," said Eddie, indicating towards the bar.

Martin thought about it for a moment and then conceded the point and signalled the barmaid to bring another round.

Chapter Seven

McGrath went through to the front office where Jackie McGhee and Sadie Agnew were sitting at their desks fielding calls from taxi customers. There was a Perspex screen separating the two desks; a token effort to keep his employees safe from spreading COVID to each other. It was a few minutes before Jackie noticed he was standing behind them.

"Oh, hi boss, I didn't see you there. Been here long?"

"Long enough to see that we're busy. Where are Mick and Pat?"

"If they're not in the back room, they'll most probably be in the Burgh Bar. They've been waiting for it to open for God knows how long. They've been going on about it for weeks!" she remarked.

McGrath nodded. "Fair enough. I'll be through the back making a few calls and I don't want to be disturbed. Understood?"

Jackie knew what that meant. She had worked for McGrath for several years and knew that he had other business interests that were not as legitimate as the taxi trade. She also knew when to mind her own business and not to ask any questions. To make matters worse, McGrath had real anger management issues and she did not want to face his wrath, not again. "Understood, we'll keep out of your way," she said and returned to the laptop which showed two calls waiting. She put on her headphones and went back to work. "Hello, Rock Taxis, can I help you?"

McGrath went through to the back office and closed the door behind him. He opened the desk drawer and took out the small mobile phone that he only used to speak to Petrie. He turned on the phone and made the call.

"Hi, it's me, you wanted to speak?" said McGrath with a slight nervousness in his voice, which only ever surfaced when speaking to Petrie.

"Ah yes, McGrath, we need to renegotiate our deal," said Petrie, getting straight to the point. There were never any pleasantries shared in these conversations; Petrie was only ever interested in doing business.

"Oh, in what way? You're not going to stop my supply are..."

"No, of course not. Quite the opposite in fact. I want to double your current supply."

"Double it? McGrath replied. He struggled to come up with a response that didn't sound quite as negative but failed. "I'm not sure I can sell that much?"

"Well, that's not my problem, is it? And it'll be cash upfront as usual," Petrie added.

"And what if I can't pay upfront? What then?" McGrath asked.

"Then we won't have a deal... and we won't be friends anymore."

McGrath hesitated for a moment to gather his thoughts. He knew he did not have enough spare cash to cover the cost of the next delivery and would need to buy a bit more time to put the money together. "Okay, but I'll need a few days to come up with the extra cash. I still haven't sold all of the last batch and..."

Petrie cut him off. "We'll deliver the goods on Monday. Usual arrangements. And you better have all the cash," he said and abruptly ended the call.

Petrie did not need to finish the sentence with 'or else'. McGrath knew all about Petrie and was aware of what the consequences of letting him down might be. "Shit," he said into the phone, which he was still holding to his ear. He was tempted to throw it against the wall and smash it into smithereens. Instead, he put the phone back into the drawer and kicked the small wire basket that was sitting beside the desk as hard as he could. Jackie and Sadie heard the racket in the front office, turned and looked at each other knowingly and then went back to taking calls.

Chapter Eight

Things were now getting more than a little bit tense in the pub as all three men sat quietly, all of them willing their last team to score the winning goal. With only ten minutes to go, Billy's selection was now showing five green home wins and one red due to a score draw. This meant they would just about break a little more than even if the result stayed the same. Billy was closely monitoring his cash-out amount as it dropped down penny by penny. He knew he had to decide sooner rather than later, this was what got his adrenaline going. He loved the risk involved but knew from experience that discipline, not greed, should be the main driver for decision-making and nothing else. With that in mind, he was about to press the cash-out button when both Eddie and Martin simultaneously jumped out of their seats with joy.

"Yes, ya wee beauty!" screamed Eddie. Billy looked down at the small screen to see the last game go to green.

Billy smiled at his two pals but knew that what he was going to do now was riskier and would not sit well with Eddie and Martin who were practically celebrating their victory as if it were a done deal. With almost seven minutes left, not including any extra time added by the ref, there was still a risk of losing the bet and so Billy looked at the total, which was now showing £22.68. If he cashed out now, he would collect more than triple his original stake of £6. Billy hit the button, put his phone down and sat back.

"What are you doing Billy?" asked Martin. "The games are still going. There's still five minutes to go..."

"Shit!" Eddie shouted.

"What?" said Martin, automatically looking at his phone, not waiting for Eddie's reply. "Aww fucking hell. Morton have just equalised!"

"Not to worry," said Billy. "You'll still get more than your stake back if it's only one match..."

"Fuck sake!" exclaimed Eddie even louder. "St Mirren have just equalised with Aberdeen."

"Ah, you'll be lucky to get your stake back if that stays the same," said Billy grinning from ear to ear.

Eddie looked up from his phone and noticed Billy's grin. "What are you smiling at? It's your loss too."

Billy shook his head. "Nope. Remember rule nine. I cashed out when all six went green. I've won £23.68."

"You crafty wee bastard," said Eddie. "You never let on..."

"I didn't see the point. You didn't have the cash-out option available to you. But it does demonstrate what my rules are all about. It's not just about picking the right matches although clearly that is part of it. It is also about knowing when to take the money and not to be greedy."

Martin frowned and looked to Eddie to respond but he had nothing. Billy could see that he had gone a bit too far.

"Don't be too disappointed. It was your first time. It took me months to work it all out and hopefully you two will get a quicker return than me. Don't forget that I lost a lot of money before I started to win it back."

Eddie nodded, reluctantly accepting that Billy was right. He went back to looking at his phone, mentally willing his two remaining teams to score the goals needed to complete his bet. Unfortunately, for Martin and Eddie, the scores remained the same until the end of the match and they both won just over £5 on their respective bets.

Martin sighed. "Ah well, you win some you lose some. You can get the beers in Billy since you're flush with even more winnings."

Even though it wasn't his turn, Billy didn't bother to argue and bought the next round. He didn't notice the attention some of the other customers in the bar were paying to his table as their loud outbursts had not gone without notice.

Chapter Nine

McGrath was still reeling from his call to Petrie. Having considered all his options, he finally decided to call Mick. "Get your fat arses over here pronto, we've got a problem," McGrath growled and then hung up the phone.

"What's up?" asked Pat who could tell Mick was a little rattled.

"Drink up. The boss wants us back in the office pronto," Mick replied, grabbing his glass and gulping down the remains of his beer.

Pat finished his beer in a similar fashion and then the two men left the pub and made their way down the High Street to the small taxi office. They were supposed to put their facemasks on when moving about the pub but neither bothered with what seemed to be a particularly stupid rule.

Sadie saw them come in and was quick to let them know that the boss was upset about something. Mick sighed and nodded. "Aye, he's just off the phone and sounded really pissed off about something. I don't suppose you know what's up…"

McGrath threw open the back door and glared at the two men. "What part of get in here pronto do you two pricks no' understand?"

Mick took a deep breath and followed his boss into the back room. Pat quickly followed Mick into the small office and closed the door behind him.

"Fucking Petrie, that's what's up!" said McGrath in answer to Mick's question.

Mick and Pat looked at each other with equal quantities of dread showing on their faces.

"Petrie?" asked Mick, finally working up the courage to speak. "What does he want?"

"He wants us to double our order and pay upfront!"

"What! When?" asked Mick, suddenly realising that they were in serious trouble.

"Monday, the usual arrangements."

"Monday! How the fuck…"

"Exactly," said McGrath as he dropped into the chair behind his desk.

"How much are we short?" asked Pat.

"I've got about three grand in the safe and with any luck we'll take in another grand from the taxis this weekend. So, I'd say we are about five grand short all in. Any ideas how we can get that sort of cash over the next two days?"

The room went silent as the three men stopped talking to gather their thoughts.

"We could always push some more of the *powder* into the street," said Pat. "It'll no' cover the full five grand but it'll help, a bit."

McGrath nodded. He had already considered that and knew that it would not be enough. "What about you Mick? Any bright ideas?"

Mick shook his head. "Not unless we rob a shop or a bookie. The risks of getting caught are high but I'd rather face time in jail than face Petrie."

"That's it," said Pat.

"What? Are you serious? We rob a bookie?" asked McGrath in despair.

"No, but we take their cash… legitimately?" said Pat.

"Have you lost your marbles?" exclaimed McGrath, who got up out of his seat and approached Pat in a very threatening manner.

Pat backed away from McGrath fearing the worst was about to happen. "Mick, did we no' overhear a bloke in the bar boasting about having a system to beat the bookies?" asked Pat, looking desperately for his mate to back him up. "An… and he won. Didn't he Mick?"

McGrath turned to Mick. "Well, Mick?"

"Well, aye or so he claimed. I couldn't really hear him that well. I think he had something written down on a bit of paper."

"Who was he, do we know him?" asked McGrath.

"I don't think so but I'm sure I've seen him in the Burgh Bar before…before COVID closed it, I mean."

"Okay," conceded McGrath. "Let's have a look at that bit of paper and we can decide if he's got something or if he's just full of shit! Right now, I'm willing to try just about anything!"

Chapter Ten

"Right Eddie, it's your round," said Billy getting to his feet. "I'm off to the loo, my bladder's busting - I'm clearly not used to having so many pints." Billy put on his mask and headed to the back of the pub.

Mick and Pat came into the Burgh Bar via the back door and immediately spotted Billy going to the toilets. Mick nodded to Pat to follow him. Pat did as instructed and then stood at the door blocking access while Mick stood at the urinal beside Billy and relieved himself. As Billy turned to wash his hands, he noticed Pat at the door and nodded. "It's all yours, pal," he said, indicating towards the vacated urinal.

"Sounds like you and your pals won a few quid judging by the noise coming from your table," said Mick, who had finished emptying his bladder and was now standing just behind Billy as if queuing to wash his hands in the solitary sink.

Billy turned towards him. "Eh, yeah, just a few quid on the football, nothing major. The boys can get a bit over excited when they've had a few beers. I'm sorry if we were a bit loud."

"Did I overhear you talking about having some sort of system...to beat the bookies?" asked Pat.

Billy was now becoming a little nervous. Pat hadn't moved from the door and was blocking his exit. "Look, I'd hardly call it a system. It's just a few rules I use to reduce the risk of losing, that's all. I've been a bit lucky!"

"Is that what is on the bit of paper you have in your pocket?" asked Mick.

Billy instinctively put his hand over his pocket. "Yeah, but as I said it's just some rules..."

"Let's have a look then," asked Pat.

Billy removed the sheet of paper from his pocket and passed it over to Pat, who quickly snatched it from his hand and read it to confirm it was what they were after.

"Do you mind if we keep this?" asked Pat.

"Yes, I mean, no I don't mind, but you need to follow..."

"Thanks." said Pat, who stuck the paper in his pocket and turned to leave.

"Hold on a minute," said Billy. "Look, I don't know who you are or what you need that for but you need to know that there will be times when you may make a loss. It won't be very often but it is possible so don't think you can just start using it and make money right away. It doesn't work like that."

"Don't you worry about that," said Mick. "I'm sure we'll be able to follow your system, sorry your *rules*, without any trouble. Oh, and if we need to speak to you about it again, I'm sure we'll see you around but just in case we don't, where do you live?"

"None of your business," said Billy.

"Oh really? Well, we'll make it our business," replied Mick who nodded to Pat.

Before Billy could respond Pat had removed the wallet from Billy's back pocket.

"Hey, give that back. What is this?" said Billy who tried to grab the wallet back from Pat. Quick as a flash, Mick punched Billy on his lower back, close enough to one of his kidneys to disable him. Billy screamed in pain as he fell to his knees, one hand holding his back, the other flat on the ground, keeping him from lying on the wet, dirty floor. He tried to get his breath back, having been winded by the punch.

Pat held up the small photographic driving licence that he had removed from the wallet. "William Taylor, 7 Barnhill Road, Dumbarton."

"Don't worry William or is it, Billy? We're not going to take your wallet or your money. Now be a good boy and go back and have a drink with your pals and forget you ever met us," said Mick.

Pat threw the wallet and driving licence on the toilet floor and the two left the pub via the back door, both laughing loudly as they went.

Billy slowly got back to his feet and went and collected his wallet and licence. He rinsed both items under a tap and then proceeded to wash his hands again. *Bastards,* he thought, *I hope you lose every penny you've got.* He gathered himself and then went back to the table where Eddie and Martin were sitting.

"What kept you?" asked Eddie. "We thought you had done a runner out the back door or something".

Billy didn't respond and sat down, wincing at the pain in his back.

"What's the matter Billy?" asked Martin.

"You know the two guys that were sitting over there, earlier? Well, they must have overheard us talking and decided that they wanted a piece of the action."

"What? Did they beat you up to get a hold of your system?" asked Martin looking concerned.

"Rules," corrected Billy. "Well, I wouldn't say they beat me up but one of them punched me in the back while I was struggling to get my wallet off the other one."

"Fucking bastards," said Eddie getting to his feet.

"Sit down, Eddie. It's alright. They've gone now so let's just forget it."

"But what about your wallet? You'll need…"

"They gave it back. All they took was the bit of paper with the rules on it and even that won't do them much good because neither of them looked smart enough to use them properly."

"Aye, well I hope they lose," said Eddie.

"Yes, that'll serve them right but the only problem is that they now know my name and address so maybe that might not be such a good thing after all. What if they lose and come after me?"

Martin was sitting quietly looking concerned. "When you said it was the two guys sitting over there. Can you describe them, Billy?"

"Aye, one was wearing a leather jacket with blue jeans, the other had..."

"A green tracksuit," said Martin finishing his sentence.

"Yes, that's them," confirmed Billy.

"I think I know who they are and worse than that, I know who they work for. And it's not good news!"

"What do you mean?" asked Billy.

"They work for McGrath, you know, Rock Taxis!" Martin exclaimed.

"So?"

"He's a fuckin' lunatic," said Eddie, who was now looking as concerned as Martin. "You really don't want to be messing with McGrath. He's done a bit of time in Barlinnie and has a bit of a reputation in this town as being a total nutter."

"And those two thugs work for him then?" asked Billy.

Martin nodded. "Aye, and they are nothing compared to McGrath."

Billy took a sip of his pint. "Well let's hope they want to use my rules for their personal gain and not McGrath's."

"Aye, I'll drink to that," said Eddie.

Chapter Eleven

Pat and Mick walked quickly back to McGrath's office, happy in the knowledge that they had the answer to all their problems on the piece of paper that Billy had so easily given up in the Burgh Bar. They both thought that he would have put up much more of a fight and were slightly disappointed that it had been so easy.

DC Jim Armstrong had followed them to the back door of the Burgh Bar and had been almost caught out by how quickly they had come straight back out. He had waited a few minutes and was just about to enter the pub when both men approached the back door, laughing as one of them held up some bit of paper as if it were a winning lottery ticket. Fortunately, he spotted them first, took out his car keys and quickly pretended to be looking for his car in the car park across the road. He then followed them on foot from the opposite side of the road, keeping his distance to avoid any suspicion. However, it quickly became obvious to him that they were heading back to the taxi office.

McGrath was waiting anxiously for the two men to return. He could hear them talking as they entered the back door and knew from their voices that they had been successful.

"We got it, boss," said Mick as he entered the room. Pat went straight over to McGrath and handed over the paper.

McGrath wasted no time in reading it and looked completely underwhelmed. "Is this it? Is this all there is?"

"Aye, that's it, boss," said Pat.

McGrath sat down at the desk and read the rules over again. "Did this guy in the pub say anything when you took the paper away from him? Was there any trouble?"

Mick replied first. "Taylor, his name is William Taylor. We have his address if we need to speak to him again."

"And was there any trouble with Taylor?" McGrath asked.

"Not really. He wasn't happy about us knowing his name and address so I had to persuade him a little," said Mick clenching his fists.

"And once you *persuaded* him to give up his name and address, did he say anything about his system?"

"His rules," Pat corrected. "He refers to them as his rules. He, eh, said something about being careful as we could lose money to begin with."

"Lose money! I thought you two said he had a system to beat the bookies. We need the money by Monday!"

Pat was rattled. "That's what he said to his pals in the pub, boss! It was only after we took the paper away that he said the bit about losing.

He could have been bluffing," said Mick.

McGrath stood up and started to pace around the room. "Okay, well maybe so, but we can't risk losing any money. Let's speak to this Taylor and find out exactly how it works."

"Good idea, boss. Do you want us to go back to the pub and bring him here?"

"No, that would cause a scene. One of you watch the front of the pub while the other guards the back. Wait until he leaves, follow him until he's on his own and then bring him in. No witnesses. Got it?"

"Got it, boss," said Mick. Come on Pat, you take the front and I'll watch the back door."

"Bring him in the back way - I don't want the girls seeing him. Understood?" McGrath instructed.

"No problem. We'll bring him in the back door but we might need to knock him out first. He's a big bloke and could put up a bit of a fight," said Pat.

"Do what you need to do but remember, no witnesses."

"Aye, no witnesses," said Mick who looked at his watch. "Come on Pat, I'll check that he's still in the pub and give you a call. Hopefully, he's not gone home for his dinner yet."

Mick left the office via the back door and Pat headed for the front door. Pat crossed over the road to the other side of the High Street and walked along towards the pub. He picked a spot where he could see the front door of the pub, took out a cigarette and started smoking while he waited for Billy to appear.

Meanwhile, Mick headed along the Quay towards the pub. He found a seat on the opposite side of the road, in between the car parks which faced the waterside, Jim and waited for Billy to emerge. This time he was followed by DC Paul Black who assumed Mick was returning to the pub but soon realised that Mick instead appeared to be waiting for someone to leave. He stayed back and crossed the road taking up a position way behind Mick's peripheral vision so that he could not be spotted. He called his colleague and updated him on the situation.

No sooner had Jim hung up the call from Paul when his phone rang again. This time it was DS O'Neill calling from the wedding reception.

"How's it going, Sarge?" asked Jim.

"Fantastic. It's some place this Cameron House. And the food is amazing. I've never tasted anything like it."

"And probably never will again, eh," joked Jim.

"Aye, it must have cost a bloody fortune and no wonder Peter and Claire only invited a few of us to join them. There's no way they could afford a big wedding here. Anyway, the boss doesn't have her phone on so she's asked me for an update. Anything happening?"

"Not a lot. McGrath's in the office and the only coming and goings have involved his two henchmen, Mick Conroy and Pat Malloy. Paul's out on foot right now following Conroy. According to Paul, it looks like Conroy is waiting for someone outside the Burgh Bar, so he's hanging about to see if anything happens."

"Could be a contact or a customer," suggested Brian.

"Could be. We'll keep an eye on things anyway and let you know if there are any developments. Enjoy your night."

"Will do. I'd better go, I think Claire's dad is preparing to give his 'father of the bride' speech - the poor guy has just swallowed down a wee dram of Dutch courage and looks a tad nervous."

Jim laughed into the phone. "Poor bloke, I hate making speeches."

"Me too," said Brian. "Anyway, I'd better go. Speak later."

Claire spotted Brian on his phone and knew he was getting an update from the surveillance team. Brian caught her eye and shook his head to indicate that there was nothing to report. She smiled back at Brian in acknowledgement but was clearly disappointed.

Chapter Twelve

The East End of Glasgow was a well-known area among Scots for several reasons; it was home to Glasgow Celtic Football Club, the Barras marketplace and the Barrowlands Music Hall, which had hosted an array of Scottish and international bands over the many years it had been open. However, in addition to all those attractions, the East End was also known for being rough and not very safe. The locals were hard and unfriendly; strangers were not made welcome, especially if they strayed into some of the most dangerous pubs in Glasgow by accident. This deprived and brutal environment inevitably bred several hardened criminals like Petrie, whose reputation had been built on pure unprovoked evil violence towards anyone who got in his way. He had built up his small criminal empire the hard way but unlike some of the other well-known gang leaders, Petrie had managed to avoid being charged with any criminal offence. Of course, from time to time, some of his minions had to take a fall and do the time but no one dared to grass on him. It didn't matter what prison you ended up inside, Petrie would get to you.

Petrie, five feet ten and built like a brick shithouse with hands like shovels, was sitting in his office above the 'Dog and Bone' pub which he had acquired during the COVID pandemic. The previous owner, Davie Wilson, was already in trouble financially before the pandemic and his situation only got worse when the lockdown came into force. With no customers and a growing list of creditors to be paid, Wilson went to Petrie with the begging bowl out. Petrie agreed to take over the public house and clear all debts owed to the brewery and the other suppliers in exchange for the deeds. Of course, Petrie wanted more than the pub and the house above it; he wanted a vehicle to launder his drug money and had spent a small fortune improving the décor and making the pub one of the best in the area, ready to reopen in style after the lockdown. Not only did it look good but the pub would be safe as no one in their right mind would dare start a fight in Petrie's pub and so as he sat upstairs listening to the noise coming up from below, he was very pleased with himself. His investment had been sound, the pub would be profitable and he now had the perfect means to hide his illicit gains. So, now it was time to up his game and really stretch his wings. He had started the ball rolling with McGrath in Dumbarton and Murphy in Greenock and would start to squeeze his other associates throughout Scotland. If he happened to take a few prisoners on his way to the top, so be it. He was more than ready and able to deal with any bumps on the road. All he needed to do was control the supply of drugs and he would succeed. Yes, other drug lords were operating in Aberdeen and Edinburgh, some as equally violent and brutal as he, but they didn't have what he had – access to the Man.

Chapter Thirteen

"Well boys, I think I've had my fill of beer. It's time for me to go home to Maureen," said Billy who stood up and rubbed his back, still sore from the sucker punch he had taken in the toilets.

"Aw stay for one more, Billy. Maureen won't mind," said Eddie.

Billy stood and stared at Eddie. "Do you not know my Maureen? I'm already half-pished. No, sorry lads it really is time for me to go. Hey, it's been good to go out again though!"

"Aye, it has," said Eddie.

"I'll stay for another," said Martin to Eddie. "But what about beating the bookies? We'll never remember all those rules."

Billy nodded. "Listen, I'll tell you what I'll do. I'll have a wee look and if I think there's a good chance of winning something I'll text you both a note of games I'm betting on. Now remember, don't be greedy and remember to cash out!

"Oh, don't worry about that," said Martin. "I'm no' going to get stung like that again."

"That's it, Martin. Okay, see you boys later," he said and with a slight stagger, Billy made his way to the front door of the pub. He suddenly realised that he had forgotten to put his facemask on but no one in the pub seemed to bother.

Pat spotted him leaving the pub and called Mick. Mick made his way through the pub, being careful not to draw any attention to himself. When he reached the High Street, he could see Pat across the road pointing to Billy, who was still on the same side of the road as Mick. Mick started walking briskly towards Billy but stopped when he saw where Billy was heading: the taxi rank outside 'G82', the local night spot. In Billy's day, it had been known as Cheers and was extremely popular at the time.

Mick quickly realised that he couldn't stop Billy getting to the rank as there were too many people in the High Street and Billy was bound to react badly when he spotted Mick. So, he followed him from a distance, as did Pat from the opposite side of the road. Billy joined the queue and got into the next taxi that pulled into the rank. Mick smiled to himself. "Got him."

It was a Rock taxi. Mick called McGrath. "Yeah, we've got him - he's in one of our taxis, plate number 118, probably heading home to Barnhill Road. Get the driver to turn around and stop at the back door. Pat and I'll meet him there and get Taylor into the office."

Billy was sitting in the back seat of the taxi looking at his phone trying to text Maureen to let her know he was on his way, a task which proved a little easier when sober. He heard the driver speaking to his controller but didn't notice the car turn around at the roundabout and head back towards the town. The car pulled into High Street and followed the one-way system around to the Quay. When the car stopped, Billy looked up from his phone.

"Hey, I said Barnhill mate. What is this?" asked Billy leaning towards the driver's seat.

"Sorry mate, but I have been asked to drop you off here?" said the driver.

Mick opened the back door of the car. "Hello Billy, our boss wants to have a word with you?" said Mick grinning.

Billy was surprised to see Mick standing there but soon understood what was happening to him and was paralysed with fear. "McGrath?" he mumbled.

"Yes, that's right but nothing to worry about. He just wants a wee chat about your so-called *rules.*"

Billy shuffled himself out of the car and slowly followed Mick into the office. Pat stayed behind him in case he decided to bolt.

Jim had spotted the taxi pull in and took some photos of the passenger leaving the vehicle. Paul, having followed Mick, had now made his way back to the carpark but kept his distance until the three men had entered the building.

"Who's the new guy?" asked Paul as he entered the car.

"Don't know, but I've got a few photos which might help us identify him when we get back to the station. We'd better hang about here in case he comes back out. Maybe I'll get a better shot of him facing us as he walks out."

"Aye, fine. Anyway, I'm starving, do you want a bag of chips or something? We could be here for a while."

"That's a great idea. I could do with stretching my legs though so I'll go, and you can wait here," said Jim. "Do you want anything on your chips? Cheese, gravy?"

"Naw, just some salt and vinegar, please. Oh, and a pickled onion, if they've got them. Thanks."

"No bother, I'll be back soon."

Paul made himself comfortable in the unmarked car, preparing himself for another long period of boring surveillance.

Chapter Fourteen

Billy entered the small office where McGrath was already seated awaiting his arrival.

"Come on in William, have a seat?"

"It's Billy."

McGrath could see that Billy was nervous which pleased him. Mick and Pat entered the office behind Billy and closed the door. Billy looked around the room and noticed that Pat was blocking the exit. Being completely outnumbered and now terrified of McGrath, thanks to Martin's description of the man, Billy decided to do what he was told to do and sat down in the seat opposite McGrath. Mick took up position on his right flank. McGrath took out a pack of cigarettes and offered one to Billy. "Smoke?"

"No thanks," Billy responded and crossed his arms. "Never started." He was surprised at how quickly the fear he was feeling had sobered him up.

McGrath lit a cigarette for himself and took a large draw. "Clever man, I started when I was eleven and can't give them up. Anyway, let's get down to business. I hear you have devised a system…"

"A set of rules…" interrupted Pat and then instantly regretted it as McGrath's eyes sent daggers in his direction.

"As I was saying, you have devised a set of *rules* designed to beat the bookies? Is that right?" McGrath took out the bit of paper and put it in front of Billy. "This set of rules?"

Billy nodded. "As I said to your two thugs… sorry, I mean, your men. They're designed to reduce the risk of losing and if used correctly…"

"Aye, that's what they said. But you *have* won money, right? You won today in the pub so explain to me how it works because all I can see is what appears to be some good bits of advice. Nothing more."

Billy took a deep breath in. "How good are you with mathematics?"

"Not the best. Why?"

"Have you heard about the law of probabilities?" asked Billy.

"I've heard of it but didn't really study much," said McGrath, laughing and looking round to Mick and Pat who also chuckled at the thought of McGrath studying maths.

"Okay then, let me try to explain it to you as best I can. The bookies use the law of probabilities to help them form the right odds to offer on any given bet. The lower the odds, the higher the chance of that team winning and of course the bookies do their homework. They gather a lot of statistics and then use mathematical formulae to calculate the odds and as you know the favourites do not always win but when applying these factors to the law of probability you can be certain that the bookies will be correct at least 8 or 9 times out of 10. Then you must factor in that most gamblers will not back a single bet as the odds would be too low to be worthwhile i.e., not worth the risk. My rules are designed to reduce the risk of losing but at the same time make it worth your while. So, one of my rules is to only bet on football matches – why? Because there is less risk than in other forms of gambling. There can only be three outcomes at a football game – home win, draw or away win so right away the law of probability works in your favour, you have a one-in-three chance of getting it right. Compare that to horse racing with as little as six horses or as many as forty horses in the big races like the Grand National. Do you follow me?" asked Billy, who was now caught up in the excitement of explaining his theory and had forgotten his first fears.

McGrath nodded, "Yes, I see the logic, but it still does not guarantee a win, right?"

"Right!" confirmed Billy. "So, I rely on the bookmakers' assumptions about a game as they will always have more information than me and therefore one of my rules is only to bet on those teams with very low odds. I've also reduced that risk further by backing home teams only as this also takes into account any advantage a home team might have in their home ground."

McGrath picked up the piece of paper and read it over again. "Okay, I see what you're saying but what's this bit about cashing out?"

"That's very important and has been the key to my recent successes. I cannot tell you the number of times I have lost money in the last ten minutes of a game. You can be sitting pretty, counting your winnings and then a team scores a goal and the return on your stake greatly reduces due to the nature of the multiplier bets. So again, that's about reducing the risk of that happening. Admittedly, it does involve using your judgement when deciding when the best point is to take the money and run but as a rule of thumb, I usually accept anything over double the stake."

"So how much have you won then?" McGrath asked.

Billy hesitated. He didn't anticipate that type of question and was unsure if he should answer or not. McGrath could sense his reluctance to respond.

"Well, you either tell me or we'll beat it out of you. Your choice." McGrath nodded to Mick who approached Billy. Billy caught the movement out of the corner of his eye and stood up, backing away from Mick. "Look, there's no need for any violence. I'll tell you. Okay!"

McGrath nodded to Mick who returned to his original position. "Okay, how much?"

"Just over a thousand pounds," said Billy.

McGrath did not look to be impressed. "Is that all? How long did it take you to win that?

"Just under three months. I only bet £6 at a time so…"

"And how often have you lost during the past three months using your rules?" asked McGrath.

"I couldn't be sure without checking but from memory I think I've only lost money on one occasion since using the rules. Most of the time my wins are small, and I rarely win the full return due to the cash-out rule but that's the discipline needed to make it work and reduce the overall risk of losing."

McGrath sat quietly staring at Billy, contemplating what to do next. Finally, he broke the silence. "Okay, here's what we are going to do - or rather here's what you are going to do. You clearly know what you're doing but just to make sure I'm going to reduce my risk by letting you pick the teams to bet on. How much credit do you have on your app right now?"

"Well, I have over a thousand as I've never cashed it in,' said Billy. His heart was now pounding at the thought of what was coming next.

"Good, I want you to gamble the lot on your next bet. It needs to be tomorrow though as I need the cash pronto."

"What? No, that's not how it works. There's too much risk – my rules say don't be greedy…"

"Mick!" said McGrath.

Mick grabbed Billy, lifted him off his seat and then punched him hard in the lower gut. Billy folded over like a rag doll and collapsed down onto the chair, both arms tucked in protecting his lower abdomen from further attack.

"Alright. Alright. I'll do it. Just keep him away from me," pleaded Billy.

McGrath nodded to Mick who immediately backed off. "Okay, so here's what's going to happen. You're going to pick six matches from tomorrow's games and text the details to me. I'm going to take a note of them and if you win you can transfer the cash direct to my bank account. What's your phone number? I'll text you my bank details."

"And what if I lose?" asked Billy.

"Oh, you don't want to do that," said McGrath. "Remember, we know where you live."

Remember! How could Billy forget? This was a living nightmare. How could such a good day out with his pals end up so badly? He now wished that he had never shared his rules with his pals in such a public place. It had all been going well; he had control over everything. He was going to surprise Maureen and treat her to a nice holiday when the pandemic was finally over but what now? He knew that if he won, McGrath would demand more and if he lost! Well, that would be worse.

McGrath stubbed out the finished cigarette in the small glass ashtray on the desk and stood up. "Pat, get the girls to organise a taxi for Billy and take him out the back way again."

Pat disappeared and returned a few minutes later. "The taxi is on its way."

"Okay Billy, give me your mobile number and you can get on your way. I'll send a text so you can save my number to your phone," said McGrath. "And by the way, no one hears about this arrangement. Got it?"

Billy nodded and gave McGrath his number. He then followed Pat outside and into the fresh air where a taxi was waiting for him. Pat opened the front passenger door. "No charge, courtesy of Mr McGrath," he said to the driver.

The driver grumbled but knew better to argue and drove off as soon as Billy got in.

Jim and Paul were still eating their chips when Billy came out and got into the taxi.

"I'm going to follow him, Paul. You stay here and watch out for McGrath."

"What about my chips?" Paul asked.

"Take them with you, ya numpty. Now, out, quickly before I lose sight of the taxi."

Paul closed the door and the unmarked car shot away in pursuit of the taxi, almost knocking the poke of chips out of Paul's hands. "Bloody hell, Jim!" he shouted and then sauntered over to the nearest bench to finish his chips.

Chapter Fifteen

The journey home in the taxi was one of the worst that Billy could remember. His stomach was churning and was still sore from the punch. His heart was pounding hard and he felt sick. When the taxi stopped Billy got out as quick as he could and immediately threw up on the pavement. Thankfully, none of his neighbours were around to see him.

The path and stairs leading up to the first row of terraced houses on Barnhill Road wound all the way up to the top of hill and were lined with a grass verge on one side and small gardens on the other until it narrowed at the top where it was surrounded by garden on either side. Billy's house was conveniently positioned on the left-hand side of the path, second house from the bottom and therefore was just a short walk from the main road where the residents parked their cars. He slowly climbed up the tarmac pathway until he reached the entrance to his front garden. He stopped to look up at the modest mid-terraced house, with its large front window and matching glass front door. They had bought the three-bedroom house just after their marriage, hoping to start a family. Much to their disappointment and upset, Maureen hadn't been able to carry a child beyond the first few months of pregnancy and so it was just the two of them living in the house that they now called home. The blinds were half closed so he couldn't see if Maureen was sitting in the living room or not. He took a deep breath, entered the house and could see that Maureen was busy cooking in the small galley kitchen which led directly from the narrow hallway.

"Hello Billy, dinner won't be long," she said without looking up. "What took you so long?"

Billy had forgotten he had sent her a text just before the taxi took him to McGrath's place and so he was now struggling to come up with a plausible explanation. "Oh, yeah, bloomin' taxi broke down so I had to wait for another one."

Maureen turned towards him, this time she looked at him face-on. "Are you alright Billy? You don't look too good. How much have you had to drink? I warned you to take it easy."

Billy decided to go with Maureen's explanation. "Yes, and you were right… as usual. I'll just nip upstairs to freshen up. Okay?"

"Okay love, don't be long," she said and went back to tending to the meal.

Billy turned and went upstairs to the master bedroom and sat on the double bed. He took out his phone and started to go through some of the games which were scheduled for Sunday. The more he looked at them the more his stomach twisted and turned. *Oh God, it's not looking great.*

"Billy! Your dinner's ready."

"I'll be right down," he shouted back down the stairs. He took off his jacket and went into the bathroom at the top of the stairs, splashed some water on his face and looked at himself in the mirror. Maureen was right, he did look terrible.

Chapter Sixteen

Jim had managed to follow Billy all the way home and drove past the taxi, which had stopped at the bottom of Barnhill Road to let Billy out. He turned his car around in one of the garage spaces and drove back down the hill just in time to see Billy enter house number seven. He took a quick mental note of the address and then headed back towards McGrath's office.

Paul was sitting on the bench watching the back door when Jim returned. Jim parked the unmarked car in a different parking place from before but still had a clear view of the taxi office. He was soon joined by Paul who slid into the passenger seat.

"Anything happening?" asked Jim.

"Nope. All quiet. How did you get on?"

"I've got an address for our mystery visitor so we should be able to ID him when we get back to the station"

"Maybe we should pay him a wee visit and find out what he's up to," said Paul.

"Better not do anything without checking with Brian first. Remember, the boss doesn't want McGrath to know that we're watching him."

"Oh, aye, right enough. I should have thought of that," said Paul.

Jim did not respond to the comment by his hapless colleague. Although Paul had only joined the team a few weeks ago, Jim was already convinced that he was not suited to detective work. Paul had been a PC for over ten years before applying to join CID and Jim had quickly concluded that Paul was better suited to his previous role, walking the beat. However, he did acknowledge that what Paul lacked in intelligence he made up for in pure brute strength and did not mind having him at his side when it came to physical confrontations. Paul was well known in local Police circles for his boxing prowess, having won several internal Police tournaments, which gained him some popularity and admiration among his colleagues in 'L' Division. Jim was convinced that it was only Paul's popularity among senior officers that had enabled him to join the CID, although he would be surprised if this impressed the DI. That said, for all DI Redding's small frame and stature, she had already proven to be more than capable of handling herself. Firstly, by breaking the jaw of a former bent copper who was now spending the rest of his days behind bars but perhaps even more impressive was how she had dealt with a knife-wielding maniac, who had not only kidnapped and killed a few locals but had stabbed DS O'Neill. 'The Keeper', as the local press had named him, had not survived the fall he had suffered after DI Redding had kicked him over the edge of scaffolding at Dumbarton Castle. Needless to say, she had been cleared of all the charges following an internal investigation and had gained the respect and admiration of all her colleagues at 'L' Division. The young DI had now set her sights on getting McGrath and Jim was confident that she would succeed. It was just a matter of time.

"I think I'll give Brian a call and see what he wants us to do," said Jim.

"He's probably as pissed as a fart by now!" laughed Paul. "Lucky sod. I can think of a few other things I'd like to do on a Saturday evening instead of being stuck here in a car with you. No offence."

"None taken," said Jim and took out his mobile phone. After a few rings, DS O'Neill responded. "That you Jim? Yes, hold on." Brian found a quiet space to talk in the corridor, outside the wedding room. "Right, go ahead Jim."

Pat returned to the office to find Mick and McGrath talking about the meeting with Billy.

"What if he only doubles the money? What then? We need five grand by Monday night," said Mick.

McGrath did not need to be reminded what was at stake if they failed to find the money in time. "I know, and I've thought about it, so here's what we're going to do. I'll download a betting app, open an account and put another grand on the same games that Taylor selects. That way, we should win just enough to cover us for Monday's delivery."

"And what if we lose?" asked Mick.

"Well, we're fucked, aren't we? But bear in mind Taylor has only lost once in the last three months and he's gambling his entire winnings this time, so he'll be well motivated."

"Not to mention, the fear of Mick kicking his head in if he loses," said Pat.

McGrath sniggered at the thought. "Aye, but it won't be Mick who does it. It'll be me."

Chapter Seventeen

Billy was sitting opposite Maureen at their small dining table which was neatly located at the back of the long lounge-dining room. He had little appetite and sat quietly, picking at his meal, as Maureen told him all about her day.

"Well, what do you think Billy?" she asked.

Billy looked up and stared blankly at Maureen. "Sorry, what was the question?"

"I knew you weren't listening. Is there something wrong with the meal? You've hardly touched it."

"No, it's fine. I'm just not feeling great, that's all. It's like you said, probably too much beer."

Maureen could sense that he was holding something back. They had been married for sixteen years and she could read him like a book. She also knew if she pushed too hard, he would clam up and say nothing. "And how are Eddie and Martin? Everything alright?" she asked.

"Yes, they're fine although Martin is convinced the bank is going to close soon."

"What? You're kidding. I know things are bad with the pandemic and everything, but I didn't think the bank would close. That's terrible. Poor Martin and Helen, they must be worried sick."

Billy just nodded in response and then pushed his plate away. "I'm not feeling great. I think I'll go have a lie down upstairs and see if it passes. Sorry... about the meal. It was fine, honest."

"Okay love, I'll come up in an hour or so and see how you are."

Billy went upstairs, closed the bedroom door and sat on the bed. He took out a wee notepad that he kept in his bedside cabinet drawer and then opened the app on his phone. He started to scroll through the lists of matches for Sunday and noted down any that fitted the criteria, determined to be very careful and not select any that looked in anyway risky. After half an hour of searching, he had identified a dozen possibilities and so he started to review each one, comparing them to the others and eliminating as he went. Fifteen minutes later, he had chosen his six matches. He reviewed them again and decided that was it. He clicked on the app to place the bet, his heart racing. He could not believe that he was about to bet all his winnings in one go but knew he had no choice and so he went ahead. However, he did not get the 'bet confirmed' message as expected. Instead, he got 'Error – bet limit exceeded!' He started to panic until he remembered that he had set a limit of one hundred pounds per bet when first setting up the app. He went into the settings in his profile and updated the limit to eleven hundred pounds, which would be more than enough to allow him to bet his full balance. Having updated his limit, the app accepted the bet and confirmed that the combined odds were 2.7 to 1. This was lower than usual for a Lucky 63 bet but was a sign of how cautious he had been when choosing his selection. He opened his messages and could see a text from an unknown number - it was McGrath who had now sent his bank details. Billy replied with details of the six matches he had chosen and took a deep breath. There was nothing more he could do now but wait, hope and pray that he won. He started to contemplate what would happen if he lost. What was the worst thing that could happen? Okay, McGrath would beat him up and he might end up in hospital, but then what? He would probably leave him alone given that his rules had failed to deliver. *Maybe losing wasn't that bad an option, after all.* Deep down he did not want to take a beating, but he decided that he would not hide; he would go to McGrath's Office and face his punishment. The more he convinced himself that everything would be all right, the better he felt about the situation.

Chapter Eighteen

Peter and Claire could not have had a more relaxing Sunday morning; they had breakfast in their lovely hotel bedroom followed by a pleasant stroll along the banks of Loch Lomond. Peter had arranged one more surprise for his new bride on their short honeymoon – a trip on the seaplane! A first for them both and after that little bit of excitement, Peter had booked a table for lunch in the Boathouse restaurant with glorious views of the Loch. The perfect Sunday.

In stark contrast, Billy Taylor's Sunday was far from perfect. Having managed to calm himself down the previous night, Billy's anxieties had returned the following morning. He hadn't slept very well and had a bit of a headache when he finally decided to get out of bed and face the day ahead.

His first match was due to kick off at noon, so he did not have very long to wait until it started. It was an English Premiership match between Manchester City, who were flying, and Newcastle United who were struggling to avoid relegation so Billy was

74

confident that this match would end favourably with a home win. Four of the other matches started at 2 p.m. with his final match kicking off at 3 p.m. It was a Bundesliga match between Bayern Munich and Vfl Bochum, another game where Billy was confident that the home side would be too strong for the opposition.

Shortly after having a light breakfast, Billy decided to go for a run to try and release some of the stress and anxiety that he could feel was slowly building deep inside him. He walked down the steep hill which led towards the A82, crossed the busy road and started jogging along the cycle path towards Bowling. On a good day he would run for about an hour, which was his usual time for a 10k, and even though the sun was shining there was a refreshing cool breeze which helped him maintain a good pace without overheating. He loved running as it usually helped him clear his mind and focus on his breathing and nothing else. For him it had always been an effective form of meditation; a good way to shed stress and anxiety, but today was different. He couldn't put aside his fears about what might happen next and although the demands of the run were helping to distract him, he could still feel the underlying anxiety building up inside him, squeezing his heart and lungs, making it harder to breathe and even harder to relax. Despite this internal pressure, he continued his run until he reached the small play park at Bowling. Checking his watch, he decided to head back home. The run may have failed to relax him but at least it had helped pass the time and he would get back home in just enough time to get a shower before the first game commenced.

McGrath was sitting at home anxiously waiting for the first match to kick off. He had put a thousand pounds of his own money on Billy's selections and was beginning to question whether that had been a wise move. He turned on his phone and opened the betting app. At precisely noon, the first of the six games kicked off. Like Billy, McGrath was also confident that Manchester City would beat Newcastle, but he was more concerned about some of the other games that Billy had picked; he hadn't even heard of some of the other bizarre European teams on the list and hoped that Billy knew what he was doing.

Maureen had arranged to go out for a drink with some of her pals and so Billy now had the house to himself. He was glad as he didn't know if he would be able to hide the pressure he was under. The first game had started, and Billy had to wait for a full thirty-five minutes to pass before he could relax a little; Manchester City had finally taken the lead and he was confident that there would be no way back for Newcastle, not now that the home team had their noses in front. Nevertheless, he would keep his eye on the game to make sure nothing changed. However, to help pass the time he pottered around the house tidying up, then did some dusting before hoovering the downstairs carpets. Maureen loved it when he did housework without even being asked so it was a win-win as far as Billy was concerned. With only five minutes to go in the match, Billy was starting to get a bit nervous; City were still only one goal up and anything could happen. He sat frozen to the spot staring at his phone willing the minutes to pass. It was torture but eventually the game ended with City winning by one goal. Billy let out a huge sigh of relief and decided to go and make himself a cup of tea while he prepared himself mentally for the other games to get underway. At 2p.m., four of the six games commenced, and although every result mattered just as much as the other Billy did not feel the same pressure that he had in the first game. The first forty-five minutes passed quickly, and Billy could see that two of his teams were winning; one by a two goal margin, the other by just one goal. The other two games were still nil-nil draws but according to the statistics on the app, both of Billy's teams were dominating possession and had more shots on target than their opponents, which was quite comforting. Everything seemed to be going to plan.

Forty minutes into the second half and things were looking good for Billy's selections; all five of his bets were green and the last game, which started at 3 p.m. was goalless. The cash-out total had risen steadily as goal after goal appeared on the screen but it still hadn't reached double the stake yet, so Billy knew he had to wait. He had decided that if his final team managed to score a goal, he would cash out immediately. With all six games showing green wins, the cash-out total would almost certainly be enough. With twenty-two minutes to go in the remaining game, Billy was beginning to feel the strain. The cash-out total which had reached £2412.78 at one point was now dropping rapidly and had now reached £1869.87. Normally Billy would have been relaxed - he was still in profit and could take his money anytime, but not today. He knew McGrath needed him to double the money and so Billy held on waiting for his team to score.

McGrath was becoming very irritated. He could also see the cash-out total reduce minute by minute as time started to run out on the final match between Bayern Munich and Vfl Bochum. Then, with only nine minutes of ordinary time remaining Bayern scored. Roars of joy could be heard in both households as the two men celebrated.

Billy looked at the cash-out total which had suddenly jumped to more than double his stake and he immediately hit the cash-out button. The app confirmed that he had won £3566.20 which was a profit of £2515.20 for McGrath. Billy was pleased with that and went to pour himself a whisky. He sat down and slowly savoured the drink which warmed his insides as it slipped down deep into his belly. He could feel the tension easing and breathed out slowly, enjoying the moment.

McGrath had decided to ride his luck and could see that if Bayern won the game, he would make a total profit of £2700 on his £1000 bet. *Not bad,* he thought. He would have enough money to pay Petrie and have some money left over. He decided there and then that his relationship with Billy was going to be more permanent.

After a few minutes, McGrath checked his phone and could see that his gamble had paid off. Bayern had won the game. Shortly after this, his phone pinged to indicate that he had received a text message. It was Billy confirming that the money would be transferred to McGrath's account, as promised.

Chapter Nineteen

On Monday morning, DI Claire Redding entered the 'L' Division Police HQ at Overtoun, Dumbarton. Her honeymoon was over. She sighed and put on her facemask, which was mandatory when moving around the office. They were allowed to remove them when sitting at their desks if they were socially distanced. The furniture in the room had been moved around to ensure there was a two-metre space between all desks. Claire was not entirely convinced that this was necessary now that they had all received their first vaccination, but the rules were the rules and she and her colleagues had to comply.

Despite the added complications that COVID had brought to the job, Claire had never been happier at any point in her life. She had just married the man that she loved and was doing the job that she loved. *What more could she ask for?*

She smiled as she entered the small CID office and was greeted with words of congratulations from

Jim and Paul. She happily showed off the small wedding band on her left hand, complemented by the more expensive diamond engagement ring which sparkled as it caught the morning light.

"Anything further to report on McGrath?" she asked, immediately getting down to business. Her team expected nothing less.

DS O'Neill turned towards Claire, remaining in his seat; he hated the whole wearing of mask thing and avoided it whenever possible. "The boys have identified a new contact. He was seen entering the taxi office late on Saturday afternoon and was there for at least twenty minutes."

"Really. Do we know who he is?" asked Claire directing her question to the two detective constables.

DC Armstrong was first to respond. "Yes, boss. I followed him home after the meeting. According to the electoral roll, William and Maureen Taylor reside at 7 Barnhill Road. I've checked and he does not have a criminal record. I also did a quick search on Facebook to find out some more about him. Apparently, he works at the Meadow Leisure Centre."

"So, what's his connection with McGrath then?" asked Claire.

"We've no idea and obviously didn't want to interview him without checking with you first - you know, in case McGrath found out we were watching him."

Claire nodded. "Good work, Jim. What do you think Brian? Should we have a quiet chat with this William Taylor?"

"I don't see the harm - we do need to eliminate him."

Claire was silent for a moment. "Has the Meadow Leisure Centre opened yet?"

Again, Jim responded. "No boss, they are all due to open in a few weeks' time, according to the website. Apparently, they're getting a deep clean before they reopen."

"That's a laugh," said Brian. "They weren't very clean before they closed. Bloody changing rooms are a disgrace."

The room erupted in laughter at Brian's off-the-cuff outburst.

"All right let's focus on the task at hand," said Claire. "Jim, Paul, I want you to continue with the surveillance on McGrath. Brian, let's pay a wee visit to Mr Taylor and find out exactly what is his connection to McGrath."

Chapter Twenty

Maureen was busy downstairs getting ready to go to her work while Billy was upstairs making up the bed when the doorbell rang.

"I'll get it," shouted Billy as he made his way downstairs and opened the door where DI Redding and DS O'Neill were waiting. "Can I help you?" he asked.

"Good morning, I'm DI Claire Redding and this is DS Brian O'Neill from Dumbarton CID. Are you Mr William Taylor?" Claire offered her warrant card as identification, but Billy didn't take any notice of it.

"Yes. I am *Billy* Taylor. What's this about? I haven't done…"

"We just want to ask you a few questions about an ongoing enquiry Mr Taylor. Can we come in?"

Billy hesitated. 'Well, it's not a great time, my wife is just about to go out to work and…"

"Oh, it won't take long and we don't need to speak to your wife. In fact, it would be better if we could speak to you alone," said the young detective.

Before Billy could respond Maureen entered the hall, grabbed her coat and made her way to the door.

"Oh, hello," she said looking at the two police officers and then turned to Billy seeking an explanation.

"They are from the police. Apparently, they want to speak to me about some investigation they are conducting."

"What? You haven't done anything..."

Claire intervened. "That's correct Mrs Taylor, we are just here to ask your husband to assist us with our enquiries. He hasn't done anything wrong. Now, could we come in? We only have a few questions..."

"Yes, of course," said Billy stepping back to allow both officers to enter the house. Just go through to the living room on the left there and I'll be right through."

"Oh, almost forgot, do you want us to wear facemasks?" asked DI Redding.

"No, you're fine. "Just go through," said Billy pointing to the room.

Maureen turned to Billy and whispered. "What's this all about?"

"Honestly Maureen, I haven't got a clue. Look, you'll be late for work. Off you go and I'll tell you all about it later. Okay?"

"Okay," she said, unconvinced. She kissed him on the cheek and then rubbed off the lipstick she had left there. "See you later."

Billy hated it when she did that. His mother used to do the same to him when he was a wee boy and he hated it then. Billy entered the living room rubbing his cheek, wondering what on earth the two police officers wanted to speak to him about. DI Redding and DS O'Neill were standing admiring a painting of Dumbarton Castle on the wall.

"Please, take a seat, said Billy. "I'm intrigued to know what this is all about."

The two officers sat down on the small sofa and Billy sat on the matching armchair opposite.

"We're here to ask you about your relationship with Kevin McGrath, owner of Rock Taxis?" Claire asked.

Billy's heart almost stopped. If he had appeared relaxed before, he certainly didn't now and both police officers could sense it. Billy was struggling for words. "I, eh, I don't have a relationship with Mr McGrath," he responded without any real conviction.

Claire knew he was lying and pushed on. "So, you didn't spend twenty minutes in his taxi office on Saturday afternoon?"

"What? How did you know that? Have you been following me?"

DS O'Neill smiled wryly at his response. "No, we were not following you Mr Taylor, but we were watching McGrath's office and you were spotted entering and then leaving the premises just after five."

Claire could see that Taylor was shocked by the revelation. "Look, Mr Taylor, it's McGrath that we're investigating so it's very important that you tell us the whole truth. We need to know why you were there."

Billy took a deep breath and explained exactly what had happened, starting with his encounter with the two thugs in the toilets and then finishing up with the discussion in McGrath's office. He didn't mention that he had transferred over two thousand pounds in winnings to McGrath on Sunday.

"So, you have designed a set of rules to beat the bookies and McGrath asked you to put on a bet for him?" And you expect us to believe that?" asked Brian.

"It's the truth, I promise," pleaded Billy.

Brian raised his eyebrows in response and waited for Claire to follow up.

"Okay. Say, we believe you. What do you think McGrath needed the money for?

"I've no idea." said Billy.

"Are you aware that McGrath deals in drugs?" asked Brian, still not convinced with Billy's version of events.

"Allegedly... deals in drugs," Claire corrected her colleague. "That's what we are trying to establish."

Billy started to panic. He could see how this was beginning to look. "Please, you need to believe me, I have nothing to do with drugs if that is what you are thinking!"

"So, you do know that McGrath's a drug dealer," said Brian.

"What, I didn't say that. You're putting words in my mouth now!"

"But you didn't deny it, did you?" Brian pointed out accusingly.

Claire sensed that Brian had rattled Billy enough and decided to change tact. "Okay, Mr Taylor. Let's go back a bit. You said that McGrath wanted you to put a bet on for him? Is that correct?"

"Yes," said Billy.

"Okay, good. How much did you bet?"

"Just over one thousand pounds."

"And did you put the bet on?"

"Yes."

"And did you win the bet?"

"Yes."

"How much did you win?"

"Approximately three and half thousand pounds including the stake."

"And where is the money now?"

"I transferred the winnings, about two and half thousand pounds, to McGrath yesterday by bank transfer. He gave me his bank account details."

"And you will have a record of all those transactions in your account confirming everything you have just said?"

"Yes, I can show you the betting app, details of my withdrawal having won the bet and the bank transfer of monies from my account to McGrath's. It's all there and as far as I'm aware. It's all perfectly legal."

"That's good. If you give your consent, DS O'Neill will take a look at those details later." Claire was now convinced she had heard the truth. "When you were speaking to McGrath did, he mention any other names or say anything which you think might help us with our enquiries?"

"Not that I can think of," said Billy.

"And did McGrath suggest that he might want you to make more bets on his behalf if you were successful?" asked Brian, who was still a bit sceptical about the whole betting system story.

"He didn't say. I hope not," said Billy.

"Well, if he approaches you again, and it sounds like that is very likely, we would be grateful if you could be our eyes and ears," said Claire, taking over from her colleague. She passed a copy of her business card to Billy.

"What, you mean... like... spy on him? You wouldn't want me to wear a wire or anything like that?" he exclaimed.

"No Mr Taylor, we wouldn't. This is not the US and we're not on the telly. Besides, that type of surveillance requires a warrant in this country, and we do not have enough evidence to justify it, yet. So, are you willing to help us? To be our eyes and ears if he gets in touch and report back if you hear anything of interest. We wouldn't want you to take any risks though, just listen and report back."

"Well, I'm not sure. What if he doesn't get in touch again?" asked Billy.

"Then you do nothing. The last thing we want is for McGrath to find out that we're onto him," said Claire.

Billy nodded. "Okay then. Do you still want to see the details on the bet and the transfer of cash?"

"Yes, if you can show DS O'Neill the information, he can take some notes."

Billy took out his phone and opened the app and passed it to Brian, who could now see that Billy had been telling the truth.

"You wouldn't happen to have another copy of your rules available, would you?" he asked.

Chapter Twenty One

Claire and Brian made their way back to the car content that their meeting with Billy Taylor had gone as well as it could. They could never force Billy to spy on McGrath but Claire could sense that although he was clearly very frightened, he just might have enough courage to help with her investigation. Only time would tell.

"Do you think Taylor told us everything that happened in McGrath's office?" asked Brian.

"I'm not one hundred percent sure about that but I am convinced he's not involved with drugs. I do wonder what prompted McGrath to bring him in though. I mean, why would he need the cash so quickly? You heard Taylor, McGrath insisted on the bet being made and paid out on Sunday."

"Yeah, the thought did occur to me, but if Taylor did know the reason, he was pretty good at hiding it," said Brian.

"Well, we can only hope that McGrath gets in contact with him again and maybe we'll get something we can use."

Brian nodded. "In the meantime, do we keep Jim and Paul on surveillance?"

"Yes, but I can't see the DCI allowing us to keep that going for much longer. We're falling behind on other work and it's not as if we have any strong leads, other than Taylor, to justify it."

"Aye, well you never know what's round the corner. Here, do you think there is anything in that system of Taylor's? I was thinking of giving it a go myself."

"There must be something in it. Look at how much he has managed to win in a short space of time. He does seem to know what he's doing." said Claire.

"Yeah, and can you imagine what might have happened to him if he lost and couldn't pay McGrath?"

"Yes, he's a lucky man."

"He is that. Very lucky, McGrath is a very dangerous individual." said Brian and started the car. He drove back to the police station deep in thought. He was going to try Billy's betting system out at the weekend. If it worked for Billy then why not him? And, best of all, it was completely legal?

Chapter Twenty Two

DI Redding and DS O'Neill arrived back in the CID office within five minutes of leaving Barnhill. The only short delay had been the right turn at the foot of Barnhill Road which could be notoriously difficult at busy times. The residents of Barnhill had petitioned the local Council to install a set of traffic lights at the junction but, as the A82 was a trunk road, there was very little the Council could do to influence the Scottish Government which ultimately had the final say on such matters and up until now had only agreed to the existing pedestrian crossing.

DI Redding sat at her desk and logged on to her laptop. There she could see the reports on any new cases which had come in over the weekend and had subsequently been allocated to her team by the DCI.

She scanned the reports and was pleased to see that there was nothing significant there; just the usual spate of drunken assaults, break-ins and other minor crimes but one did take her notice. A twenty-year-old Caucasian male had been arrested with a sizeable amount of cocaine in his possession. He had been taken into custody and interviewed by two officers from DI McBride's team over the weekend before being charged and released on bail. Just as Claire was going to share the information with Brian, DCI Miller entered the room sporting a colourful designer facemask. "Good morning, Claire. How was the wedding? You certainly got the weather."

"We certainly did, and the wedding was perfect. Thank you. Everything went to plan, and we had a great time. Peter even had a special surprise for me – we went up on the seaplane and did a tour of the area. It was fabulous."

"Oh, I've always wanted to do that. You lucky devil! Anyway, can we have a quick catch-up in my office? Did you see the possession charge I sent through to you?"

Claire turned towards her screen and nodded. "Yes, I was just about to let Brian know about it. I think we should follow up on it and see if there's any link to McGrath."

"That's what I wanted to speak to you about. Come on through to my office."

Claire promptly put her facemask on and followed her boss out of the office. Brian immediately went in search of the report on the possession charge and started to read the details.

Claire sat down opposite DCI Miller, who immediately took off her facemask and placed it on her small wooden desk. Claire did likewise. She now felt at ease with the DCI which had not always been the case. Claire had won the trust and respect of the DCI when she solved the mystery of 'The Keeper' which had reflected well on the whole of the CID unit in Dumbarton. From that point onwards their relationship had improved, and Claire had been given more freedom to investigate cases the way she wanted, with very little direction from her superior.

"So where exactly are we with McGrath?" asked DCI Miller.

Claire updated her on the surveillance team's report and gave a detailed account of her interview with Billy Taylor.

"So, this Taylor thinks he has devised an unbeatable system and has caught the attention of McGrath?"

"It looks that way," said Claire.

"And you think there is no connection to drugs as far as Taylor is concerned?"

"No, I don't believe there is which is why I think Taylor may be able to help us."

"Yes, providing McGrath gets in touch with him again," said the DCI. She took a moment to consider what to say next. "Listen, Claire, I'm as keen as you to nail McGrath and get him and his thugs off the street but you still haven't got any evidence to connect him to the increase of drugs that we are seeing in the area."

Claire wasn't surprised and went into defensive mode. "I know, but I feel we're getting closer. He's bound to make a mistake and when he does, we'll be there as long as we maintain surveillance on him and his gang."

"I'm concerned that your team are falling behind Claire. I've already re-assigned a few of your other cases to DI McBride's team and he's not too happy about it."

"I know and I really appreciate it. I do. Give me until the end of the week and if nothing happens, we can reduce the surveillance."

"No Claire, I will give you until the end of the week and if you have nothing by then the surveillance ends, understood."

Claire knew when to give in. "Yes, Ma'am."

McGrath entered his taxi office at 11 a.m. He had arranged for Mick and Pat to meet him there to go over the arrangements for the meeting with Petrie's men. Petrie never showed up in person when drugs were being handed over; he wasn't that stupid.

Mick and Pat were waiting for him in the back office both buzzing about Billy. They had both put money on the bet and, of course, both had won.

When McGrath entered, he was smiling and clearly relaxed now that he had the money to pay Petrie in full. "Hello boys, everything alright?"

"Couldn't be better, boss," said Pat. "What about that Taylor, eh? It worked; his system bloody worked. Mick and I made a few quid on it but nothing like what you made."

McGrath smiled at the two men and took a large envelope full of cash out his pocket, putting it on the table. He then opened the small office safe and took out the rest of cash, counted it out and handed it to Mick. "It's all there. Mick, can you double check it? I wouldn't want to upset Mr Petrie."

"No problem, boss." Mick took the pile of cash, sat down at the desk and started counting it rhythmically, first into hundreds and then into thousands. It's all there, boss."

"Good, now about tonight - same arrangements as before, we all meet up at Overtoun House. There's no lighting and never anyone around at that time of night, so should be safe enough. We stay in the car until Petrie's men arrive. When they get out, we get out. Mick, you hand over the cash. Pat, I want you watching Petrie's men. Take a weapon, just in case they try anything on. I'll take the package from them and do a quick taste test. All going well, we'll be out of there in five minutes. Oh, and no drinking before we get there, understood? We all need to be alert."

"Sure," said Mick. "No drinking... eh, I know we must do this drug lift tonight but now that we can make money legally why should we continue to take the risk of selling drugs?"

McGrath nodded. "I've got to admit I've been thinking about that myself but I just can't see how Petrie is going to let us just walk away."

Pat decided to put his tuppence worth into the conversation. "I know this is going to sound a bit mental but what if we just hand over the business to

Petrie to run himself? You know, take out the middleman, and keep all the profit to himself."

"You know Pat, you're not half as daft as you look," said McGrath.

"Thanks, boss."

"So, are we going to do that then, hand over the business to Petrie?" asked Mick.

"I need to think about it, but we'll need to speak to Taylor again. I would want to be sure that we can rely on him before we do anything drastic."

"I'm sure he could be persuaded," said Mick grinning.

"Aye, I'm sure he could but I'd rather that he was a willing partner. Perhaps, if I offered him a cut of the winnings, we could get him on board?" suggested McGrath, thinking out loud. "Let's get him back in here for a chat but this time no rough stuff. In fact, I'll send him a friendly text. Thanking him for sending the cash and inviting him for a drink to celebrate our success."

"Sounds like a plan, boss," said Pat.

"Right, okay, but first things first. Let's get tonight over and done with and then we can think a bit more about handling Taylor."

Chapter Twenty Three

Claire and Brian had spent most of their day looking at other casework and trying to progress it as much as they could but with little success. The surveillance team had also had a quiet day with only Mick Conroy and Pat Malloy being reported as entering and leaving the office. McGrath had left the office shortly before the surveillance shift had ended and so Claire decided that nothing would be achieved by continuing the surveillance that evening.

She turned off her laptop, grabbed her bag and headed for the door. "See you tomorrow, Brian," she said.

Brian looked up from his laptop and checked his watch. "Is it that time already? I'll need to go in a few minutes - Agnes wants me to pick up something nice for dinner on the way home. I think that meal at the Cameron House has changed her ideas on cooking."

Claire smiled as she relived the memory of the wedding day. "It was good, wasn't it? See you tomorrow and give my best to Agnes."

"Will do," said Brian.

It didn't take Claire very long to make her way home. She and Peter were still living in Peter's house (now their house) in Dumbarton East but they had started to talk about moving. The mid-terraced house was big enough for them but they both agreed that a house with a bigger garden would be better, especially if they started a family. Claire had stopped using contraception a few weeks back and was now happy to let nature take its course. She was in no particular hurry but would welcome the baby if and when it arrived. Peter on the other hand was dead keen to get the family started and had reassured Claire that he would give up his job to take care of their child, which suited Claire. In stark contrast, he was bored with his job and was looking forward to taking a break from stock-broking.

Claire arrived home and found Peter in the kitchen with Sally, his black and white Cocker Spaniel. Having greeted them both with hugs and kisses, she then went upstairs to get changed for dinner. As usual, Peter had started to prepare the evening meal; he often got home before Claire, who was normally late but not tonight. Claire came back into the kitchen wearing jogging bottoms and a plain white t-shirt. "Can I do anything to help?" she asked, looking over Peter's shoulder to see what he was preparing.

Peter turned his head and promptly kissed her on the nose, missing her left cheek which had been his intended target.

"Aw, yuck," she said, pulling back and wiping her nose clean.

"Sorry," he said, laughing at her antics. "You can chop an onion if you want to be helpful. It's just plain old mince and tatties, I'm afraid."

"Sounds good," said Claire.

"You're in early today - slow crime day in Dumbarton, was it?" he asked jokingly.

"Something like that," she responded.

"And how are you getting on with our local drug dealer?" he asked.

Claire had decided some time ago that she could share information about her work with Peter. He was a good listener and often looked at things differently from her, which had on occasion helped her to solve a crime or two. He was also a bit of a loner with no friends or family outside of their own small circle so there was nobody he was likely to share anything with. That aside, she knew she could trust him. After all, he had saved her life once before.

"McGrath? Oh, nothing really but I must tell you about a bloke we interviewed this morning. He seems to think he has produced a gambling system to beat the bookies."

"He's talking rubbish. There's no such thing. Gambling is a mug's game."

"Yes, well he thinks he has and has drawn the attention of McGrath."

"You're kidding. He's playing with fire if McGrath's half as bad as you say."

Claire went silent, now questioning if she had done the right thing by asking Billy to help her. "Yeah, well, he did win a small fortune for McGrath first time round."

"Oh, well in that case maybe he's got something. You can tell me more about it over dinner." Peter took the chopped onion over to the pot and added it to the mince which had browned nicely. He added some more water and some seasoning to the mix and put the lid on the pot and allowed it to simmer gently on the hob. Peter's mince was never plain.

Peter loved his mealtime conversations with Claire. Her work was fascinating in comparison to his desk job and way more difficult and dangerous than he ever imagined it would be.

They sat down at the small dining table which looked out into the back garden. Claire explained the betting system in as much detail as she could remember and tried to answer some of Peter's more technical questions but was acutely aware that his mathematical brain was more suited to understanding how the system worked.

"It's certainly a very clever way of reducing the risk of losing," Peter concluded. "I'm just not convinced that you are guaranteed a win every time. The cash-out feature is interesting though. I'd never heard of that before and I can see how it could make a difference."

"So, you don't think it's as good as Tay... as this guy thinks." She stopped herself from saying his full name. It was one thing to name a well-known thug in-person but another to name an innocent informant.

"It does sound like he knows what he is doing. After all, he has had success, but how much of that success is down to his personal judgement and skill?

"So, if someone like McGrath were to try it out himself it could end in disaster."

Peter nodded as he chewed another forkful of food before responding. "Yes, and if I were McGrath, I'd want to make sure that my money was safe before taking any risks.

"That's exactly what he did. He made this guy use his own cash so he couldn't lose."

Peter looked up in surprise. "Really? He used his own cash to fund McGrath's first bet?"

"I don't think he had any choice. It was either that or take a severe beating."

"I wouldn't like to be in his shoes now. There's no way someone like McGrath is going to let go now. Why would he?"

"That's what I'm counting on," said Claire. "That's exactly what I'm counting on."

Chapter Twenty Four

The exchange had been arranged to take place late on Monday night. The roads were more or less empty of traffic and there were no police cars actively patrolling the quiet streets of Dumbarton. The remoteness of Overtoun House, nestled high up in the hills behind Dumbarton, had proven to be the perfect spot for their illicit deals.

McGrath and his team got there first. They drove around the grounds of Overtoun House to make sure no one was around and parked in their usual spot waiting anxiously for Petrie's men to arrive.

Petrie's men arrived just after eleven o'clock and parked next to McGrath's Volvo; his sporty Audi TT was far too small for three large adults.

McGrath looked round at Mick then Pat. "Right, stick to the plan. Let's go."

Pat patted his jacket pocket where he kept his gun - checking that it was still there.

Mick went to the back of the Volvo as planned, opened the boot and took out the envelope with the cash.

Digger, the smaller of Petrie's two men, looked around slowly before opening his boot. "So, you managed to get all the cash after all? Just as well!"

McGrath ignored the comment. "It's all there. You can count it if you want."

"Oh, no need for that. You wouldn't be here if you didn't have *all* the cash. Hand it over then."

McGrath nodded to Mick who in turn handed the cash over to Digger. He threw it in the boot and took out the two heavy parcels of cocaine and handed them to McGrath. "I suppose you'll want to check it out?" asked Digger.

McGrath nodded in response and removed a small pen knife from his jacket pocket. He pierced each packet carefully taking a very small sample and touched his tongue with the white powder. Immediately, he knew that the product was good. He nodded to Mick and Pat and then closed the boot of the Volvo.

"Oh, by the way, Mr Petrie asked me to pass on a wee message. The next drop will be double again."

Mick was first to react. "What the fuck, we'll never move that much..."

McGrath put his hand up indicating that Mick should stop speaking. He noticed that Digger's larger partner's hand immediately went to his pocket searching for his weapon.

"It's okay Mick. Leave it, Pat," said McGrath, now looking at Pat who also had his hand in his pocket, clearly pointing his gun towards the big man. "Pat, take it easy." McGrath turned towards

Digger. "You can tell Petrie that I'll be in touch with an even better offer. Now piss off back to the shit hole that you came from."

It was clear from the expression on Digger's face that he was caught out by the response. He had been expecting some form of resistance to Petrie's proposal but not this.

"Fine, I'll pass on your message but it better be a good offer, Petrie doesn't like surprises." He nodded to his partner and they both got into the car and left.

McGrath turned to Mick and Pat. "Well, it looks like Petrie has made our decision for us. We need to get out now before the situation gets any worse. I'll offer him the business for nothing as I'm pretty sure that's what he wants anyway. He must know we can't move that much powder so quickly."

"So, how do you want to handle Taylor?" asked Mick.

McGrath smiled for the first time that night. "Oh, just leave Taylor to me. I'm sure we can come to some form of understanding."

Chapter Twenty Five

Billy Taylor sat in his living room deciding whether to answer the phone. He had recognised the number on the screen as soon as it appeared. Deep down, he knew that it was only a matter of time before McGrath contacted him. Just as he had worked up the courage to speak to McGrath, the call went to voicemail. "Shit, too late!" he said out loud to the empty room. He waited a few minutes for the voicemail message to be confirmed by text and played the message.

"Hi Billy, it's McGrath here. Can we meet to have a chat, I have a proposal for you."

Billy was taken aback by the tone of the call. McGrath was not anywhere near as aggressive as he had been when they met in his office. In fact, he almost sounded friendly. *Proposal?* Billy wondered what McGrath had in mind this time. Clearly, it had to do with gambling but the 'proposal' suggested that there would be something in it for Billy other than a beating. Billy also knew that if he contacted McGrath, he would need to let the police know. He felt trapped and knew he did not have much choice in the matter. He found the business card that the attractive young detective had passed to him and made the call.

"Hello, is that DI Redding?" he asked.

"Yes, who is calling?" responded the familiar voice.

"It's Billy Taylor - McGrath's been in touch."

Chapter Twenty Six

Billy chose to drive down to see McGrath. They had agreed to meet at 3 p.m. and Billy was still in the dark on what exactly the 'proposal' would entail but, having spoken with DI Redding, he felt a lot less pressure on his shoulders - whatever the outcome, he would not end up in jail.

He parked at the back of the taxi office in the Quay car park and made his way towards the back door as instructed by McGrath. Pat was standing there waiting for him and ushered him through to the back office to where McGrath was waiting. Billy was relieved to see that there was no sign of Mick and was even more pleasantly surprised when McGrath asked Pat to leave the room so the two could talk in private.

"Please sit down," said McGrath pointing to the chair in front of him. "Would you like a drink?"

Billy would have loved a stiff drink at that point but he had to keep his wits about him. "No thanks, I'm driving."

"Quite right," said McGrath who poured himself a large whisky from the bottle and sat down. "Well, firstly, I just wanted to say thank you for sending over the cash so quickly. I must admit that I had my doubts about your wee system… I mean rules, but now that we've got the first win under our belts I wonder if you would be interested in helping me make a bit more money? Of course, this time you would also benefit."

DI Redding had told Billy to play hard to get and not jump in and accept the first offer to avoid any suspicion. "What do you mean that I would also benefit?" Billy asked cautiously.

McGrath smiled with pleasure. "What I mean is that I am willing to put up the stake this time and if we win, then I will give you ten percent of the profits."

"So, I pick the teams, control the bet and only get ten percent? That doesn't sound very fair."

"Well what percentage do you think would be fair?" McGrath asked with a little less enthusiasm and a little more hostility in his voice.

"Fifty percent, we split the profits evenly," said Billy.

McGrath laughed at the ludicrous suggestion. "Nice try, but it's my money. I take all the risks. Twenty percent," said McGrath, becoming more agitated.

"Thirty percent and we have a deal," said Billy.

"Twenty-five percent and that is my final offer."

Billy hesitated. He could tell McGrath was about to explode and decided that he had pushed him far enough. "Okay, twenty-five percent."

"Good, I'll need some time to gather in some more cash before our next bet. What's the best day to put the bet on?"

Billy was about to ask what had happened to the winnings from the previous bet but thought twice about it. "Saturday, there's more games to choose from."

McGrath hadn't really thought about it before now but could see the logic in the answer. "Of course, makes sense. Right, so you pick the teams. Text them to me, same as before, and I'll put the bet on using my app with my cash this time. Sound okay?"

"Yeah, but I'll need to monitor the bet and tell you when to cash out. Remember the rules?"

"Oh, how could I forget," said McGrath sarcastically. "There's nothing to stop you putting some of your own money on the same bet. That way you can tell me when you have cashed in your bet."

"Never thought of that. Of course, I will. How much do you intend to bet this time?" asked Billy.

"As much as I can pull together before Saturday. That's where Mick is now – out making little collections."

Billy knew exactly what he meant and didn't push for an explanation.

The surveillance team had spotted Billy leaving the taxi office and immediately noted the time on their record.

As soon as Billy got into his car, he called DI Redding.

"Hello, DI Redding, Dumbarton CID," she answered.

"Hello, it's Billy Taylor. I've seen McGrath and set up another bet for Saturday."

"That's good Billy. Did he suspect anything?"

"No, I don't think so. I haggled over my share as you suggested and he reluctantly agreed."

"That's good. Well done. Did he say anything else of interest?"

"Not really, but he says he needs to gather some more cash before Saturday. Is that useful?"

"I don't know, might be. Anything else?"

"Oh, he mentioned that Mick was out making *little collections*. I think he meant selling drugs."

"Oh, is he now? That is helpful, Billy. Excellent work. Okay, keep things nice and simple with McGrath, don't do or say anything to ruffle his feathers, just play the game and keep us informed."

Billy felt a great weight lift off his chest. "Thanks, will do," he said and hung up.

Claire put down her phone and immediately called over to DS O'Neill. "Brian, we might just have a break in the case." She told him about Mick being out and about, potentially selling drugs and started to discuss the best way to approach it.

"Do we know what vehicle Conroy drives?" asked Claire.

Brian quickly reviewed some of the reports submitted by the surveillance team. "Yes, he has a white VW Golf, registration number BD17 SKT."
"Good, let's put out an alert to all cars in our area to start looking for it. Tell the surveillance team to check his home address in case he's still there. No need to watch McGrath's office for now, let's just focus our efforts on Conroy." She paused to gather her thoughts. "Hold on, let's not pull him in if we do find him. Let's wait and see who he deals with and then pull them instead."

"Sounds like a plan boss, but only if we find him. He could be anywhere," said Brian.

"I know but it's all we have for now. We should be out there too, in separate vehicles to increase our chances of finding him."

"Okay, I'll let Jim and Paul know what we're doing." He picked up his phone and called DC Armstrong.

"Hi Jim, It's me. The DI wants you to go to Mick Conroy's house. If he's there, wait and if he moves, follow him."

"No need Sarge, Mick returned to the taxi office a few minutes ago; he was in one of McGrath's taxis. He was also carrying a poly bag."

"What? Hold on a minute, Jim."

Brian waved over to Claire to get her attention. "Boss, cancel the alert, we've got Conroy. The bad news is that he has returned to the taxi office so he might have finished his drug run."

112

"Okay, tell Jim to stay there and to follow Conroy if he leaves the office. Hopefully, he's just dropping off some cash."

"Will do. Oh, by the way, he is using a taxi and not his personal car so we would not have found him even if he was still out and about."

"Well, that ties in with the anonymous tip-off - they did say that McGrath was using taxis to peddle the drugs."

Brian nodded and then passed the message onto Jim. He gave a clear instruction that Conroy should not be pulled in, even if he did make another drop. The surveillance team were to photograph the exchange if they could, but more importantly they should try to identify the buyer and report back to the boss.

Chapter Twenty Seven

"What the fuck does that mean?" asked Petrie.

"Don't know boss," said Digger. "He just said he had a better offer and would speak to you about it."

"It had better be a good one or else that wee bastard is a dead man. Who does he think he is? Anyway, I'll call him later. Right now I need you and Bull to make a wee trip to Inverclyde. It's time to put a bit of pressure on that wee turd, Murphy. I want you to tell him to his face that if he doesn't pay me in full for the last batch of powder, I'm going to burn his house down while him and his family are in bed. And, if he or any of his boys give you any bother then Bull has my permission to have a bit of fun - but no killing. Not just yet. Understood?"

"Yes, boss. I can't wait to see the wee Irish prick's face when I give him your message."

"Right on you go and I'll deal with McGrath."

Digger left Petrie's office and made his way downstairs to the pub to find Bull. Petrie picked up his phone and called McGrath. The phone rang a couple of times before McGrath answered. He knew it was Petrie's number and gathered himself before swiping the green button on the small screen.

Mick Conroy left the taxi office less than ten minutes after he had arrived. He had dropped the cash off with McGrath and then caught up with the girls in the front office. He fancied Sadie and never missed the chance to chat her up. However, the feeling was not mutual and Sadie did her best to ignore him.

He had one more drop-off to make today and would hopefully collect enough cash for the next big bet on Saturday. He was quite excited about it and could not wait for the weekend. He also knew that if the win was big enough McGrath would hand over the drugs business to Petrie and hopefully that would be the end of the matter. However, his gut told him otherwise.

Mick drove up to Bellsmyre and parked his car at the far end of Merkins Avenue, opposite the high block of flats where his buyer was eagerly awaiting his visit.

DC Armstrong and DC Black parked a little further down the street.

"Shit, it looks like the deal is going down in one of those flats," said Jim. "You wait here, and I'll follow

Conroy into the block and find out which flat he enters."

"That's a bit risky. What if Conroy spots you?" asked Paul. "You know what the boss said about that."

"I know but what choice do I have? If we know what flat he enters with the goods then we have grounds for a search warrant. The boss wants the buyer, so I'll need to risk it."

Jim waited until Conroy entered the close and quickly ran up to the outer door. He peered through the glass panel to see if Conroy was waiting outside one of the two ground floor flats but could not see him, so he very carefully opened the door trying to avoid making any noise. Fortunately for him the door was relatively new and opened without any fuss or noise. He crept to the bottom of the close staircase and looked up to see if he could see Conroy but had no success. *Where in the name of hell has he gone?* Jim decided to make his way upstairs then stopped suddenly at the sound of a knock on a door. He moved to the wall of the stairwell and crept up step by step and stopped again when he heard the door open. He had reached the second landing and knew from the direction of the sound that Conroy had entered the third floor flat on the left. When he was confident that the door had closed, he went up to the landing and had a quick look for a nameplate. There wasn't any.

Jim took a note of the flat number and went back to the car where Paul was anxiously waiting for him

"Well, did he spot you?"

"No, don't think so. He's in a third-floor flat. No name on the door but it's flat number 3/1. Call the boss and let her know what's happening." said Jim.

"No need. I've already called and told Brian what's happening. He says if you get spotted, you're back to wearing the uniform."

"Just as well I didn't then," said Jim. "Anyway, let's call in the address and find out who rents the flat. We're going to need that search warrant."

"So let me get this straight, McGrath. All of a sudden, you want to hand over your business to me. No pay-off. Nothing. Do you want to explain why?" asked Petrie.

"To be honest it's because you keep doubling the supply. We just can't cope with that amount of powder and sooner rather than later you are going to take the business from me anyway so to save both you and me any trouble, I'm throwing the towel in now - getting out while I still can. I'll still have the taxi business. That'll be enough to keep me going. And you will get all my contacts in Dumbarton. All my buyers and distributors."

"Whenever anyone starts a sentence with 'to be honest' I know they are either lying or holding back some of the truth," growled Petrie.

McGrath ignored the accusation. "What have you got to lose? I'm offering you all my business for nothing."

Petrie paused for a moment. Taking over the business in Dumbarton had been his goal all along but there was something wrong with how quickly McGrath had capitulated. Something else was going on here. He was sure of it. "Okay McGrath, we have a deal but if you try to fuck me over you are a dead man. Do you hear me? A fucking dead man!"

"I hear you loud and clear Petrie. So how do we do this?"

"I'll send Digger and Bull over to your place. You can give them all the details about how your business works, contacts, buyers, delivery routes and so on and we'll take it from there."

"Is Bull that big mother fucker who accompanied Digger on the exchange?" asked McGrath.

"Aye, he is and he's the big mother fucker who will fuck you up right good and proper if you dare cross me," said Petrie and hung up the call.

Chapter Twenty Eight

Two hours after Mick had left the flat in Merkins Avenue, DI Redding and DS O'Neill had managed to get a warrant to search the premises and had met DC Armstrong and DC Black outside the property. They were accompanied by two uniformed officers, one of whom was carrying what was affectionately known as the 'hammer' in police circles but took the appearance of a small metal battering ram: perfect for opening locked doors quickly.

Claire quickly assessed the block of flats and gave her instructions. "Jim, you go round the back to spot if they try to throw anything out of the back windows. Paul, you stay down here at the front. Brian and I will enter the flat with the help of our two uniformed friends here. Okay, are we all clear on what we are doing?" She didn't wait for a response. "Right, let's go then."

The party of four police officers made their way upstairs to the door of the flat. Claire rattled the letter box to get the attention of the occupier. She could hear someone approach the door and stop. "Who's there?" asked the male voice behind the closed door.

"Police... we have a warrant to search these premises. Open the door."

As soon as Claire stopped speaking, she could hear bolts sliding into place. "Bolts," she shouted and stood aside for the officer carrying the hammer to do his work. It took three blows of the hammer before the door frame gave way and the police officers rushed into the narrow hallway. Claire looked quickly in each room and found a man in the bathroom trying to flush the small packets of powder down the toilet but without much success; the light polythene bags floated on the surface of the water. He was in his early twenties, had long dark brown hair and was unshaven. Some might have described him as being ruggedly handsome but Claire didn't think so. All she could see in front of her was another pathetic little drug dealer who didn't give a damn about the lives that were ruined by drugs.

He heard Claire enter the room and panicked, his eyes searching desperately for an escape. Claire read his mind. "There's nowhere to go unless you want to jump out that small window over there, but I don't fancy your chances. So why not turn around and let my colleagues put a set of cuffs on you? And then we'll have a wee chat about the content of those little bags you were so desperate to flush away."

Brian entered the small bathroom and immediately saw the man and the bags floating in the toilet and shook his head in disbelief at the stupidity. "There's no one else here, boss. He's on his own."

"Good," said Claire. "Put a set of cuffs on him and bring him into the living room. I'll let Jim and Paul know we've got him. They may as well go back to McGrath's and keep watch in case anything else happens."

Claire made the call and then joined Brian in the living room with his young prisoner. "Sit down Raymond, I just want to have a wee chat," she said to the nervous young man. If Raymond was surprised that she knew his name, he didn't show it.

"So, Raymond," she repeated. "You have been caught red-handed trying to get rid of the drugs and judging on the quantity you have in your possession I think you are going to have a very hard time persuading the Fiscal that they were for personal use."

She was hoping for a reaction to her statement, some form of denial or defence but there was nothing, so she tried again. "And of course, Raymond, this is not your first time, is it? Your sentence won't be as light the third time round. It will be hard time in Barlinnie for a repeat offender like you. No chance of community service this time... not unless you fully cooperate with us and, if you do, we will put in a good word with the Fiscal, won't we DS O'Neill?"

Brian smiled at Claire, acknowledging the invitation for him to join the conversation. "Come on son. Do yourself a favour. Tell us who supplies the drugs and it'll be a lot easier for you."

"I'm not going to say anything without a solicitor. I know my rights," he said, and then stared out the living room window, trying to avoid making eye contact with either of the two officers.

"Of course, you are quite correct," said Claire. "But we haven't charged you with anything yet. Have we DS O'Neill?"

"No boss, no charges have been made and no rights have been read out to young Mr Lynch here."

"There you go, Raymond. No charges have been made and no rights have been read. We're all just having a friendly chat trying to get to the bottom of this whole big mess that you find yourself in."

This got his attention. "So, I'm not under arrest then?"

"Not yet!" said Claire, sensing that they were getting somewhere.

Raymond sat there thinking about his next move and made up his mind. "Well, I still want to speak to a solicitor."

"Fine, if that's the way you want it, Raymond. DS O'Neill, please ask our two constables to escort Mr Lynch to the station and get him his solicitor. We'll carry out a quick search of the premises in case there are any other surprises hidden away for us to find and join him back in the station as soon as we can."

Chapter Twenty Nine

Petrie looked out of his office window, which was directly above the Dog and Bone, and spotted Digger and Bull entering via the front entrance below.

About bloody time! He was keen to find out how they had got on and as soon as they came into the room, he demanded a report on the meeting with Murphy in Inverclyde.

"It's all good boss," said Digger. "Murphy had the money ready and cash counted out before we got there."

Digger took out the cash from his inside pocket and placed it in front of Petrie. "He didn't seem very happy about it though so I warned him that if he was late again there would be consequences."

"So, no trouble then?" asked Petrie.

"Well, not with Murphy but on our way out one of his boys squared up to Bull here. He was a big fella, just like Bull but, well… let's just say he won't do that again in a hurry."

Petrie laughed and looked at Bull who just raised his eyebrows and said nothing. "Okay, well done but I think we may need to up the pressure on Murphy sooner rather than later and see how tough he really is."

"No problem, boss," Digger replied.

Petrie walked over to the window and looked out into the busy street below. "Now, let's talk about McGrath. Apparently, he is ready to hand over all his business and just walk away."

"What? That's good news right. Just what we wanted? Right boss?" asked Digger.

Petrie turned to face the room and sat on the wooden windowsill. The light from behind him outlined his sturdy figure, illuminating him as if he were a god and he certainly felt like one at this moment in time. "Yes, but why so quickly? We hardly put any pressure on him."

Digger nodded. "So, how do you want us to play it?"

"I told him that you and Bull will pay him a wee visit to learn all about his business, but I also want you to see if you can find out what is really going on there. There's something not right, I can sense it."

"No problem, boss. Leave it to me. We'll get in touch with McGrath and set up the meeting, face to face."

Chapter Thirty

"Right, Raymond, now that you've had a chance to speak to your solicitor, have you had a chance to think over our little chat in your flat?" asked Claire.

She was sitting beside DS O'Neill in Interview Room 1 facing Raymond Lynch and his solicitor, Robert Strange.

The experienced solicitor was the spitting image of Donald Dewar: his light brown hair was thinning, his large square framed glasses perched on his long bent nose, his ill-fitting jacket sitting awkwardly on his rounded shoulders.

Strange adjusted his glasses, looked down at his notes on his little yellow legal pad and spoke without looking up. "DI Redding, I understand my client was offered a deal before formal charges were made against him, is that correct?"

Claire knew from the tone of the question that she would need to be careful in her response. "As you know Mr Strange, the police are not able to offer deals but I do admit that I offered to speak with the Procurator Fiscal on your client's behalf providing he fully co-operates with us."

Strange smiled at the detective's clever response. "That's a bit unethical Inspector, don't you agree?"

"No, I was being open and honest with your client and meant every word I said and incidentally, the offer still stands... if your client is interested. But, just to be clear, Mr Strange. Your client was caught red-handed trying to flush a substantial number of drugs down his toilet. The bags were retrieved and have been sent away for analysis. I'm sure the results will not only confirm that your client had in his possession a considerable quantity of class 'A' drugs but we will also find traces of his DNA and fingerprints on the bags if we're lucky. This is the third time your client has been caught in possession of drugs and you know that the Procurator Fiscal is unlikely to look favourably on these charges unless your client fully cooperates with our enquiries and helps us to put away the real criminals who supply these drugs to small time dealers like your client."

There was silence when Claire stopped speaking. DS O'Neill loved interviewing with his DI, especially when faced with smart-assed lawyers who thought they could defend the indefensible and get away with it. She was as cool as a cucumber under pressure and could speak better than any Inspector that he had worked with over the years.

Strange cleared his throat. "Thank you for clarifying your position, Detective Inspector. My client has informed me that he is willing to fully cooperate with you providing all the charges against him are dropped."

"Come now Mr Strange, you know better than I do that that's just not possible. The best your client can hope for is that the Procurator Fiscal agrees to present reduced charges to the court on the basis that your client co-operated fully with the police. Reduced charges mean a reduced sentence." She deliberately left the carrot dangling for a moment or so. "Do you want some more time to speak to your client, Mr Strange?"

"Yes, that would be helpful," he said looking round to Lynch who was looking less than happy with the way things had gone."

Claire stood up and was quickly followed by Brian. "Okay then. We'll give you two a few minutes to talk it over. Interview suspended at four fourteen p.m." DS O'Neill turned off the recording device on the desk and followed his DI out of the room.

"Well boss, you certainly put him in his place," said Brian.

"Yes, but I'm not convinced Lynch is going to co-operate. Did you see the look on his face when I refused to drop the charges? We need him to point the finger at McGrath and be prepared to give a statement. That's the key to getting the warrant to search his premises and nail him. So far, all we really have is Mick Conroy dropping the drugs off at Lynch's place. If we pull Conroy and he refuses to give up McGrath, then Conroy goes down and

McGrath walks away a free man to set up elsewhere.

Claire looked at her watch. "Okay, they've had enough time to talk it over. Let's go back in and see what happens."

Chapter Thirty One

The last two days had almost been a return to normal for Billy Taylor. He had done his bit for the police and had heard nothing since his last report on his meeting with McGrath. No news was good news as far as he was concerned. He had also selected the next six games to bet on and had texted the details over to McGrath, who thanked him in reply and said he'd be in touch to let Billy know how much he intended to bet. Part of Billy was excited about the prospect of winning a twenty-five percent share of the profit but another part of him was nervous about what would happen if this was the week that his rules would let him down and they made a loss.

Billy had also sent the same information to Martin and Eddie, who had agreed to meet him in the pub on Saturday. Both were very excited about the prospect of winning and Billy feared that they might not have followed his advice on placing small bets.

He had also decided that it was time to tell Maureen about his gambling habit but not about McGrath. He was keen to take her on a nice holiday now that the COVID restrictions were being lifted but he couldn't spend that type of money without her becoming suspicious and so he sat there, in the front room waiting for her to return home from work, thinking carefully about what he was going to say and how he was going to say it. He knew she would never approve of his gambling but hoped that she might soften when presented with the amount of money he had made from it. Only time would tell.

DI Redding and DS O'Neill were back in the interview room with Raymond Lynch and his solicitor, Robert Strange. DS O'Neill turned on the recording device and DI Redding did the usual announcement confirming for the recording that the interview had recommenced with all four present.

"Now then Raymond, you've had a chance to speak with your solicitor. Have you decided to cooperate with us?"

Lynch shook his head.

"For the purpose of the recording Mr Lynch shook his head indicating a negative response to the question," said Claire. "Okay, then. We will proceed to ask our questions and see where that takes us. Go ahead DS O'Neill.

"We know that Mick Conroy delivered a package to your flat today. We followed him and saw him enter your premises with a package and leave your flat without it. Do you know who Mick Conroy works for Raymond?"

"No comment."

DS O'Neill opened the brown folder in front of him and looked at the A4 sheet it contained. He could see that Lynch was unsettled by it. "Is this the first time Mick Conroy has visited your flat, Raymond?"

Lynch paused before speaking. "I don't suppose there is any point denying it. You probably have the details on that piece of paper."

It was an old trick that DS O'Neill had used on many occasions. The paper contained details of Lynch's previous convictions and nothing else.

"And are you willing to admit that the package contained class 'A' drugs?"

"Well, if you mean cocaine, then yes. Why not, you caught me with them."

Claire was surprised by the sudden admission of guilt and decided to intervene. "Raymond, a few minutes ago you told us that you were not willing to co-operate but now it seems you are doing just that. You have also admitted that Mick Conroy supplied you with drugs and that he has done this on more than one occasion but you state that you do not know who he is working for. Is that correct?"

"Yes," he replied.

"So, you expect us to believe that you do not know where the drugs come from?"

"Yes." Lynch was looking cockier by the minute.

Claire decided to change direction. "Do you know what type of car Conroy drives?

"No, he always comes in a taxi."

"A taxi?" asked DS O'Neill, feigning surprise. Which company?"

"Rock..." The words came out of his mouth before he could stop them and Lynch knew he had fallen into a trap.

"That would be Rock Taxis, owned by Kevin McGrath?" asked Claire.

"I don't know," said Lynch.

Claire could see the fear on Lynch's face and decided to press on in the hope of a breakthrough. "Well, Raymond, we know that Kevin McGrath owns Rock Taxis and we also know that he has a very violent reputation." She could see the perspiration build up on the young man's forehead. All his composure and all his swagger had gone. "In fact, we have two officers sitting outside his office right now. Watching and waiting. Do you know what they saw while sitting there?"

Raymond shook his head and turned to his solicitor for help. Strange shrugged his shoulders in defeat. He had advised Lynch to be quiet and say no comment to all questions but Lynch thought he knew better and was now paying the price.

Claire read the signal and continued. "Well, it turns out that Mr Conroy was spotted returning to the Rock Taxi office in the same taxi as he was seen driving away from your flat." She paused to let this information sink in. "So, we have a direct link from your drug drop to Kevin McGrath. What do you think Mr McGrath will say when we bring him in and question him about all this Raymond?"

Strange decided it was time that he should intervene and try to protect his client, albeit a bit late in the day. "Is that a threat detective?"

Claire smiled at Strange. "Mr Strange, I think when you play back the recording you will find that it was a question to Mr Lynch and not a threat. I should also point out that your client denied knowing Mr McGrath or any connection with his taxi business a few minutes ago. Can you explain how my question could be considered a threat if your client has no knowledge of Mr McGrath? Judging by his demeanour, I have the feeling that your client was not being completely truthful."

By this point, Lynch had had enough and was fearing the worst. Not only was he heading off to prison but long before that would happen, McGrath would tear him apart. In stark contrast, Brian was enjoying himself and was doing his level best to hide his pleasure at the young man's discomfort.

"You're not going to tell him, are you?" asked Lynch.

"Tell who Raymond?" asked Claire knowing full well who he meant.

"McGrath, and yes, I know of him; he's a lunatic. You've got to protect me. He'll kill me if he finds out."

"Just to be clear, are you now admitting that it was McGrath who provided you with drugs?" asked Claire.

"No, no, I never said that. I know of him, and I know he's a lunatic."

"Well, here's the thing Raymond. The only way we can protect you is if you are willing to give evidence against McGrath. That's why it's called witness protection."

Chapter Thirty Two

If Billy had been confident about telling Maureen about his gambling earlier in the day that confidence had slowly dissipated the closer it got to her coming home. He was becoming increasingly nervous about her reaction to the news and he could not make up his mind about how he was going to approach it.

He was in the kitchen making dinner, which had become the norm since she had returned to work. He was looking forward to going back to work - the boredom of being at home had gotten to him and he had had enough.

Maureen arrived home just after five. "Hello Billy, that smells good," she said entering the small kitchen.

"Hello love. It's *coq au vin*, I've also got some roast veg in the oven. Should be ready in about ten minutes."

"Great, I'm starving." She went to the cutlery drawer, collected what she needed and went through to the dining area to set the table.

"Fancy a bottle of wine?" Billy shouted through to the living room.

"What, on a work night?" she feigned. "Oh, go on then."

Billy brought through two plates of food and could see that Maureen had already opened the wine and had poured herself a large glass, which was what he was hoping.

"This is nice. So, what's the occasion?" she asked.

Billy took a sip of wine and decided it was time. "I've got a bit of a confession to make. During the lockdown I was bored and so I decided to start gambling..." She started to interrupt him but he decided to keep going. "I downloaded a betting app onto my phone and... well I lost a bit of money... at first but..."

"I knew you were up to something," she said, smiling at him. "Did you think I wouldn't notice the wee transfers from the joint account to your personal account? I'm not blind you know, just surprised how long it took you to confess. Anyway, the withdrawals stopped a while back, so I decided not to mention it."

Billy was flabbergasted. "Well, the thing is Maureen. I haven't stopped."

"What? What do you mean? Where's the money coming from then. Certainly not the joint account, I would have noticed that. Oh Billy, you haven't borrowed it, have you? Please tell me that is not what you're about to confess?"

"No, I didn't borrow it. I started to win."

"What do you mean?"

"Exactly that, I've started to win and actually, I've got a proposal."

Maureen was completely confused. "A proposal?"

"How would you like to go away somewhere nice on holiday this year?"

"Well Billy, that would be very nice of course, but... how much have you won?"

"Over one thousand pounds, so far," he said proudly. "And more to come now that I've accumulated enough of a stake to make some more," he said confidently.

"Whoa. Wait a minute. You mean you are going to keep on gambling, now that's... that's just stupid. You've been a bit lucky Billy, great, but come on your luck is going to run out sooner or later and you will end up losing the lot."

Billy suddenly realised that he had said nothing about his rules and went on to explain in detail how he had managed to accumulate so much money. He didn't have the heart to mention McGrath's involvement and knew that would be the final straw.

Maureen listened patiently as Billy explained the whole process. When he stopped speaking, the smile had gone from her face.

"Well Billy, I'm glad you've told me now. I really am and I can't wait to go on holiday but I want you to promise me that you'll stop gambling before it's too late. Please Billy, will you promise me that you'll stop?"

Billy nodded his head. "I promise."

Chapter Thirty Three

DI Redding had called her team in for a morning briefing to discuss their tactics to search McGrath's home and office premises. The DCI had agreed with Claire that they had now enough evidence to request the warrant and approval had come through later that night.

"Okay, is everyone listening? Good. The plan is to hit the home and office simultaneously to make sure there's no chance of McGrath getting a tip-off and moving the drugs while we search one of the premises, so there will be two teams. I'll take Paul with me to McGrath's office and Brian and Jim will take his home. I've arranged for two dogs to be available to assist with the search for drugs but remember we're also looking for evidence of the supplier. McGrath is getting his drugs from somewhere and I want to know who is behind this. Both teams will also have two PCs to assist with the search. I'm just waiting for the DCI to confirm who has been allocated and then we'll get on our way. Everyone clear on what is required?" Claire looked around the room and could see all heads nodding. "Good. Let's get ready."

Claire returned to her desk and started to gather her paperwork when her phone rang.

"Hello, DI Redding, Dumbarton CID," she said.

"Good morning DI Redding. Detective Superintendent Dan Mulholland from the Regional Organised Crime Team here."

Claire recognised the name as soon as she heard it. DSup Mulholland or 'Dutch' as he was known to his colleagues, was one of the key officers who had been involved a highly successful cyber operation to disrupt the behaviour of several criminal gangs throughout Scotland and had been heralded nationally as one of the major Police Scotland successes of 2020.

"Good morning, Sir, how can I be of help?" she asked tentatively.

"I understand you sent some samples of cocaine to the central lab for analysis yesterday. Can you tell me how you obtained these samples?"

"Yes Sir, they were taken from a batch of drugs seized from a local drug dealer that we have been investigating for a few weeks now. There has been a marked increase in the local supply of cocaine and we're trying to stop it at the source. May I ask what your interest is in this case and how did you find out about our samples?"

"Of course, it's a bit sensitive though. You see the lab was asked to flag if a certain batch of cocaine was received and it appears your batch

140

matched the cocaine that we have been looking for."

"Right, but what is so sensitive about it?"

He hesitated. "Well, it appears that your samples match samples taken from a large consignment of drugs which was seized by my team. I'm embarrassed to admit it but this batch of drugs managed to disappear just before they were scheduled to be destroyed."

"You're kidding. Someone stole these drugs from the secure area in Govan. How on earth did that happen?"

"We don't know yet which is why we have asked the lab to keep an eye out for any cocaine submitted for analysis. It appears that the chemical make-up of your supply is an exact match for the missing drugs."

"Really? Okay, I can see why this is so sensitive," said Claire.

"Yes, and I would appreciate it if you kept that bit to yourself for now. However, it would be very helpful if you could tell me who had these drugs and where they came them from?"

"Of course, Sir, we seized them from a known low level dealer, Raymond Lynch in Dumbarton, but we believe a local thug called Kevin McGrath is the supplier. Lynch all but admitted it during an interview although he was too frightened to confirm it. However, he did give us enough to obtain a search warrant, which we are just about to serve on McGrath."

"Right, good work detective, keep me posted on the outcome of the search as this could be the connection we need to retrieve the missing drugs before it goes public."

"Of course, Sir. I was going to inform the ROC Team once we had enough evidence to nail McGrath but obviously, we need hard evidence to link him directly to the drugs. It's not enough to proceed on hearsay."

"Absolutely. Well, it seems you have everything under control DI Redding, so just keep me informed if there are any other further developments. Good luck with the search."

"Thank you, Sir. Will do," she said, and ended the call. She quickly checked her watch and looked around the room. The four PCs she had been promised had arrived and were being briefed by DS O'Neill.

He turned around and saw that Claire had ended the call. "What was that all about?"

"Oh, nothing really. Just the ROC keeping an eye on our interest in McGrath," she said.

"Really?" asked Brian. "What's their interest in a local dealer? It's hardly organised crime."

"I don't know," she lied. "They were just looking for an update on our progress. Is everything in place?" she asked, changing the subject.

"Yip, the dog handlers are waiting for us at the two sites and as you can see our PCs have arrived, so we are good to go."

"Thanks Brian. Okay, let's go."

Chapter Thirty Four

McGrath lived in one of the newly constructed detached villas on Castle Street, Dumbarton, just a short distance from Dumbarton Castle. DS O'Neill shuddered when he saw the outline of the castle. The last time he was there he had been stabbed and if it hadn't been for the timely intervention of Claire he could have died there and then, high up on the scaffolding.

"Are you okay Sarge?" Jim asked.

"What? Oh yeah, I'm fine, let's go wake McGrath up and make his day."

The two CID officers, followed closely by their two uniformed officers and the dog handler, approached the front door of the large five-bedroom house. McGrath's Audi was parked in the driveway along with a silver Volvo. Brian took out the search warrant from his jacket pocket and knocked loudly on the door. Before he had the chance to knock again, the door was opened by Kevin McGrath, fully dressed. Brian was a little disappointed.

"Mr Kevin McGrath?"

"Yes."

"We have a warrant to search these premises. I'm Detective Sergeant O'Neill and this is Detective Constable Armstrong." Brian handed over the warrant to McGrath who read it over and handed it back to Brian.

"I don't know what you expect to find here but I suppose you better come in and have a look since you've gone to all this trouble. However, I have one condition," said McGrath, looking down at the feet of the two detectives, followed by the two constables and the dog handler standing further down the path.

"And what would that be?" asked Brian, confident that he was about to tell McGrath to fuck off.

"I've just had new carpets fitted throughout the house, so if you don't mind taking off your shoes, you're welcome to come in."

Brian looked down at his shoes - it had been raining heavily the night before and the streets were still wet. "Fair enough," said Brian. The last thing he wanted was a bill for carpet cleaning being sent to the DCI.

"You can all leave your shoes and boots here on the porch," said McGrath and walked back into the house as if he didn't have care in the world.

DI Redding's entry to the taxi office had proven to be somewhat more straightforward than the entry to McGrath's home. The front door of the taxi office was open and a member of McGrath's staff was already in there dealing with calls. When presented with the warrant, Sadie read it over and moved aside to let them enter the premises.

"Is it okay if I let Mr McGrath know that you're here?" she asked.

"Of course, go ahead," said DI Redding. "My colleagues are searching his home as we speak so he'll be fully aware of our interest in his business. Where is Mr McGrath's office?"

"It's through the back. I'll need to get the key. He always locks it at night."

"I'm sure he does," said Claire, hoping that McGrath had been careless and left behind something of use to her investigation."

Sadie opened the door to the back room and let the two detectives into the office. The other police including the dog handler started searching the rest of the premises. Claire began searching through the desk, which was the obvious place to keep any paperwork while Jim moved from wall to wall, checking behind the picture frames.

"Look boss," said Jim, removing a large picture of a stag from the wall and placing it carefully on the floor. Claire stopped searching the desk and approached the neat little wall safe that the picture had been concealing.

Jim tried to turn the handle. "It's locked."

"No surprise there," said Claire, who then went back through to see the taxi operator.

"Sorry to interrupt... eh... sorry what was your name again?"

"Sadie."

"Yes, sorry Sadie, do you have the key to the safe next door?"

Sadie looked shocked at the request. "No, I don't, but I'm not sure Mr McGrath would want you to get access to his safe. He keeps a lot of commercially sensitive documentation in there, or at least, that's what I've been told. The safe is off limits to everyone but him."

"So, he must have the key then?" asked Claire.

"Well, yes, I suppose he must."

"Okay, thanks." Claire took out her phone and called Brian.

DS O'Neill was busy in an upstairs bedroom going through a set of drawers. So far, he had found nothing of any interest and was beginning to doubt if he would. McGrath had appeared to be relaxed about the search, which was unusual. "Hi boss, what's up?"

"We've got a locked safe here but no key. One of his staff says that McGrath has it. Can you ask McGrath to hand it over to one of your PCs and get them to drop it off to me as soon as possible?"

"Will do boss," said Brian. "We've not found anything here yet. The sniffer dog has been all over the place and found nothing so we're now looking for other evidence but it's going to take a while; it's a big house.

"Same here. Oh, don't forget to check his cars. The warrant covered all his property including his vehicles."

Brian could have kicked himself for being so stupid. "Of course, boss, was just about to do that. Leave it with me and I'll call you back about the key."

Brian went downstairs and found McGrath sitting on a large sofa, checking his phone messages. He looked up as the detective entered the room. "I understand you are also searching my taxi office, Detective. Nice of you to let me know."

Brian ignored the dig. "We'll need the key to your office safe and also the keys to both cars in your driveway."

McGrath stood up and faced Brian. "I don't suppose the word *please* appears anywhere in your vocabulary?"

"Please," said Brian and put out his hands to receive the keys.

"The car keys are in the hall but I want to be present when you open my office safe. Just to make sure *your lot* don't plant anything in there. Wouldn't be the first time, would it?"

Brian didn't have a clue about what McGrath was referring to. "I'm sure that can be arranged. If you wait here, I'll ask one of our constables to escort you to your office, providing you have the key."

"I have it here," said McGrath. He reached into his trouser pocket and produced a long brass key.

"Fine, wait here." Brian went out into the hall and then into the kitchen where PC Johnson was busy searching. "I need you to take Mr McGrath to his office, right away. Where's the dog handler?"

"He's out in the garden searching the shed."

"Right, thanks," said Brian. He went to the back door and called out to the dog handler who stopped what he was doing and quickly made his way to the backdoor.

"Find anything," asked Brian.

"Nope, just finished with the shed and found nothing of interest."

"That's a pity. Okay, we'll need to search both his cars as well. "I'll get the keys. Sorry, but you can't come back in here with those dirty shoes," said Brian pointing down to the handler's muddy shoes. "You'll need to go round the side of the house, I'll meet you at the front."

Brian went through the house to the hallway where PC Johnson was just about to leave along with McGrath.

Brian found the car keys on the hooks on the wall behind the door and stepped outside, where the dog handler was now waiting for him. Brian pressed the open door buttons on each device and heard the doors unlocking. "That's them opened now. Let me know if you find anything."

"No problem, come on Scout," said the dog handler to the young Cocker Spaniel and opened the door of the small Audi TT to let the dog do its job.

PC Johnson and McGrath arrived at the taxi office. The young policeman opened the back door, let McGrath out of the car and followed him into the building.

"Morning Sadie," said McGrath, striding right by her and making his way into the backroom where Di Redding was waiting patiently.

"You must be Kevin McGrath," said DI Redding. She recognised him from the many photographs they had on file back in the station. "I'm Detective Inspector Claire Redding. I assume you have the key to this safe?"

McGrath stopped to look at the petite detective with some amusement. He had read the stories in the Lennox Herald about the brave young detective who had taken down the "The Keeper" but was surprised by her diminutive stature.

"That's why I'm here – to make sure *you lot* don't plant anything in there," he said, with more than a little venom in his tone than was necessary.

Claire was slightly taken aback by his attitude. Brian had not let on that McGrath was such an arsehole. "Oh, I think you've been watching too much telly Mr McGrath. You shouldn't believe everything you see," she said patronisingly. "You see, here in the real world, we like to do things by book. Anyway, if you wouldn't mind opening the safe then we will *all* be able to see what you have in there."

149

The dog handler had finished his search of the Audi and found nothing, so he moved on to the bigger Volvo. Scout started sniffing around inside the vehicle but it was only when his handler opened the boot did Scout start to react to something. The handler looked carefully inside the boot and could not see anything obvious. Nevertheless, he knew from Scout's reaction that there had to have been something of interest in the boot. Reluctant to take his shoes off for the second time that morning, he called out for DS O'Neill from the doorway. "Sarge, I think we've got something."

On hearing the call, Brian ran quickly down the stairs eager to hear the news but nearly slipped as there was very little friction between his socks and the new carpet. Luckily, he managed to grab the handrail and stopped himself from going down on his backside.

"Fuck me, that was close," he exclaimed. "So, what's the news?"

"I think we need to get a SOCO to check out the boot of the Volvo. I can't see anything obvious but Scout certainly thinks there's been something in there, don't you boy?" Scout barked excitedly in response.

"Good work," said Brian. "I'll let the DI know and get a SOCO down here right away."

DI Redding stood aside to allow McGrath to open the safe. It was empty.

McGrath turned and smiled. "There you are detective. As you can see it's empty. I always empty the safe last thing at night and deposit the day's takings in the bank over the road before I go home."

It was a plausible explanation but Claire was not willing to leave it there. "So, where are all the commercially sensitive documents that you store in there? Do you have them at home?"

McGrath knew right away that Sadie must have shared that piece of knowledge with the detective. "Oh, come now detective, this is just a wee taxi business. What commercially sensitive documents could I possibly have in my possession?"

Another good answer. Before she could think up a fitting response, her phone rang. She looked at the screen and could see it was Brian. "Sorry Mr McGrath, I need to take this call in private, so if you don't mind."

"Mind? Of course, I mind, it's my fucking office!"

Claire ignored his little ill-tempered outburst. "We've still to complete our search of *your* office so, if you don't mind." Claire signalled to the door.

McGrath was livid and made a move towards Claire only to be abruptly intercepted by DC Black, whose speed and strength surprised McGrath.

"Come on now Mr McGrath, be a good boy and do as the DI says. There's no need for any trouble. Let us do our job and we'll be out of your way in no time."

McGrath gathered himself, turned and left the office.

"Hi, Brian, what's up?" Claire smiled to herself as he relayed the news to her. At last, they had something to go on. Hopefully, forensics would confirm that there were traces of illegal drugs in the boot of his car but she also knew that this would not be enough to get the conviction of drug dealing that they were after; they needed to find a large quantity of drugs to demonstrate that McGrath was dealing. However, it was a start and after the initial disappointment of the empty safe, she would happily accept that.

"Paul, get the dog handler to come here after he's finished with the house. Who knows what we'll find?"

Chapter Thirty Five

The search of both premises had been disappointing. The Scenes of Crime Officer had taken samples from the boot of the Volvo but had not found anything elsewhere, including inside McGrath's office. The samples had now been sent to the lab for testing and Claire knew that it could take a few days before the results came back. She had decided not to let McGrath know that they had found anything just yet - not until they had the results. She was prepared to be patient; once she had the evidence needed to get a conviction, she would bring him in and put pressure on him to reveal his supplier. She knew that it was very unlikely but it was all they had. At the very least McGrath would go back to Barlinnie and his local network would go down until someone else stepped in to fill the gap in the market.

So, the following morning, DI Redding called the team back in to discuss their next steps while they waited for the results. The surveillance team would continue to watch McGrath's movements until the weekend in the hope that something would break. There was always the possibility that Billy Taylor would overhear something during his dealings with McGrath. In the meantime, DI Redding and DS O'Neill were working through the backlog of work. Claire was keen to make a dent in it while they had the chance but was finding it hard to keep motivated. Her mind kept wandering back to McGrath and then it occurred to her - she hadn't updated Mulholland on her progress. She left the office and went out into the empty corridor to make the call.

Mulholland saw who was calling him and accepted the call immediately. "DI Redding. Good morning, how did you get on with McGrath?" he asked.

"Morning, Sir. Sadly, not as well as we had hoped. We didn't find any large quantity of drugs at any of his known premises but the SOCO did find some traces of a powder in the boot of his car which we have sent to the lab for testing."

"So, not really enough for a conviction?" he asked.

"No, not for dealing anyway, not yet, but clearly we're waiting on the results of the tests and if we can match what we find in his car to the batch of cocaine seized from Johnson and Lynch..." She didn't have to finish the sentence.

"Then you would have enough to put him away. Good work Claire."

"Thanks, and of course, that might help you to track down who is behind the stolen consignment of drugs."

"Yes, it would. I assume you haven't shared this information with anyone yet?"

"No, of course not. I gave you my word, Sir. You can trust me."

"Glad to hear it, Claire. There have been a few leads at this end which I'm looking into but until I have something more solid let's just keep it to ourselves for now."

"Of course, Sir," she said and ended the call.

Brian came out of the office, heading towards the exit.

"Where are you going?" Claire asked.

"Dumbarton Academy. Apparently, they had a break-in last night and there's been a bit of damage. Want to join me?"

"No, you go ahead and handle it yourself. I've got a pile of paperwork to catch up on."

"Will do. Shouldn't be too long, probably a bunch of school kids acting up."

"Right. Well, let me know how you get on," said Claire, who promptly returned to her desk and started to wade through the backlog of emails in her mailbox.

Chapter Thirty Six

McGrath, accompanied by Mick Conroy, had arranged to meet Digger and Bull in the Red Lion pub in Yoker. The Red Lion was situated almost halfway between Dumbarton and Glasgow and therefore was considered to be neutral territory. McGrath had decided that it would not be safe to hold the meeting in Dumbarton - not now the local Police were on his case, and so both parties had agreed to meet elsewhere. McGrath had insisted that the meeting should be held in a public place; he still did not trust Petrie and knew that Petrie's men would not attempt anything stupid or risky in a public place.

Digger and Bull were already seated in a booth at the back of pub when McGrath arrived. He acknowledged the two men and sat down opposite them. McGrath took the first ten minutes to explain to Digger how his operation worked and he then provided a typed sheet of paper containing all his contacts.

"This is everyone that I deal with," he began. Locations and numbers, it's all there, so when do you want to take over?"

"That's no' for me to decide, it'll be for Mr Petrie to decide when and how," Digger replied. "I know this much, he's no' very happy about the police taking an interest in your business."

"And I'm grateful for the tip-off but they found nothing. So, there's no risk."

Digger scoffed at the response. "No risk, are you serious? You have the cops searching all over your house and business and you think there's no risk. Whit planet are you on? Come on Bull. I've heard enough of this bullshit."

The two men stood up and walked away.

"Well, that didn't sound too promising," said Mick scratching his unshaven chin.

"No, it didn't. We can only hope that Petrie sees that I'm serious about handing over the business and makes a quick decision. I knew that the police involvement would upset him but they were after me, not him, and found nothing. If we sit tight and don't take any more risks, then hopefully the police will lose interest."

"Yeah, but will Petrie see it that way?" Mick wondered.

"I hope so, for all our sakes," McGrath responded wearily.

Chapter Thirty Seven

Billy Taylor was at home doing some housework. He had promised Maureen that he would stop gambling and was now regretting confessing. He hadn't thought for a moment that she would make him promise to stop completely, a promise he knew he couldn't keep. Not when he had just made the deal with McGrath. How could he back out of that without ending up in the hospital or worse still, dead? He had considered keeping the promise in part; he would continue identifying bets for McGrath but would not gamble himself and would not accept any of McGrath's profits. However, he wasn't sure how well McGrath would receive the new arrangement. He was sure to become suspicious. Billy decided that he needed to speak to DI Redding before doing anything. He needed to know if they were close to bringing him in and if so, how long would he need to continue the arrangement with McGrath. He finished hoovering the lounge and made the call.

"DI Redding, Dumbarton CID, can I help you?"

"Hi, it's Billy Taylor."

"Hello Billy, what can I do for you?"

"I was just wondering if you were making any progress on the case against McGrath?" asked Billy.

Claire could sense some apprehension in his voice. "Are you okay, Billy? Has anything happened?"

"No, eh, well, yes. It's Maureen, my wife. I told her all about my gambling and she wants me to stop."

"You didn't say anything about McGrath, did you?"

"What? No, I'm not that daft but I'm not happy about continuing to gamble on McGrath's behalf. Are you any closer to getting him off the streets?"

"Look, Billy, I'm not at liberty to share any details with you but I can tell you that we're very close and hopefully within a few days we'll have enough evidence to charge him so I need you to hang in there a little longer. Can you do that?"

"I suppose so... I have already provided him with my selection of games to bet on this Saturday so I'll need to see that through but I'm keen to put an end to this."

"Billy, believe me, I understand and I'm sorry. I can't do any more to help you at the moment. I'll let you know as soon as we have McGrath in custody, okay?" Claire had hoped that would be the end of the conversation and waited for Billy to respond. There was silence and the call went dead.

Chapter Thirty Eight

It was Saturday afternoon and Claire was at home with Peter and Sally. They were preparing to have lunch with her mum and dad when the call came in. Peter immediately recognised the ringtone of her police mobile, which he had insisted was to be different from her personal phone to avoid confusion. He had suggested the theme tune to 'Line of Duty', the highly successful police drama about corruption in the police force. Claire, on the other hand, did not appreciate the irony or humour in his suggestion and, much to his annoyance, opted for one of her favourite pop tunes instead. He sighed as Claire put the phone to her ear but knew that it must be important as the station would not call during the weekend.

"DI Redding," she said identifying herself to the caller as was the home protocol.

"DI McBride here, the forensics have come in on the drugs found in McGrath's car. They match the samples taken from the Lynch case. There's no doubt about it. It all came from the same supply. We've got him."

"That's brilliant news. Listen, I'm just about to have lunch with my folks but give me an hour or so to get organised and then I'll come in to deal with McGrath. Oh, can you give DS O'Neill a call and let him know I'll meet him at the station? I'm sure he'll take great pleasure in bringing McGrath in - I got the distinct impression that they didn't get on very well the last time they met."

"Are you sure? You're not on duty this weekend. Mike and I can pick him up and…"

"And take all the credit! Aye, that'll be right," she said, imitating McBride's stereotypical Glaswegian accent.

"Okay, no problem. It's your case, Claire," he said chuckling to himself.

Claire hung up the phone and went back into the kitchen where Peter was waiting anxiously to hear what was going on. "Please tell me you're not going to leave me to have lunch with your parents?"

She was pleased he hadn't been eavesdropping on the conversation. "No, I'll stay for lunch but I will need to go shortly after… if that's alright?"

"Why, what happened?"

"We've finally got McGrath," she said with clear delight on her face.

"That's great. I suppose your parents won't hang about much if you're not going to be here."

"I thought you liked my parents?" she asked, deliberately changing the direction of the conversation and putting Peter on the defensive.

161

"You know I do, your dad's great and your mum, well she's your mum…"

"What about my mum?" she said, smiling at his discomfort. "She thinks you are the best thing since sliced bread."

"I know, it's just… oh I don't know. I find it hard to talk to her. She seems to think that I'm this brilliant stockbroker who has swept her daughter off her feet and…"

Claire put one of her fingers to his lips to stop him speaking. "There's no need to say anymore. I know she can be a pain. So, thank you for putting up with her and me… well, my work."

Before he could respond she kissed his lips, gently at first and then more passionately. The moment was rudely interrupted by the ringing of the doorbell, quickly followed by Sally's excited bark.

"That'll be them then," said Peter.

Claire smiled up at him and gently pushed herself away from his embrace. "Sorry, but that's all you're getting for now."

Peter immediately picked up on her meaning, smiled back and nodded. "For now," he repeated.

Petrie and Digger were sitting in the corner of Petrie's pub having a pint and discussing what to do next. The pub was still closed and Petrie's staff were busy getting ready for the doors opening. This was the only time when Petrie sat in the public bar; he couldn't stand the noise when the pub was busy, full of arseholes who couldn't hold their drink and talking shite.

"I'm sorry boss but it just doesn't feel right to me. McGrath was far too keen to give up his business and for what? Nothing! Who does that? He even gave me a written note of all his contacts and routes."

Petrie nodded. He agreed with Digger's gut feeling, it just didn't feel right. "Have you heard anything from your contacts in Dumbarton? Any rumours? He might just be panicking now that the polis are on his case?"

"Who? McGrath? I don't think so and he was quite relaxed about the whole polis thing when I spoke to him the other day. No, there's something else going on. I can sense it."

"Well, if there is, he's a dead man!" said Petrie. He took out his mobile to make a phone call and indicated to Digger that he wanted to be left alone. Digger got the message and left Petrie in peace.

Two minutes later, Petrie found Digger at the other side of the pub and told him to get Bull. The plan had changed.

Billy's Saturday had started reasonably well. His first two games were going to plan and his next four were scheduled to kick off at three o'clock. He had been very careful not to let Maureen see that he was checking his phone - the good news was that she was going out shopping soon so there would be less risk of him getting caught. Maureen finally made it out of the door just before the three o'clock games were about to kick off. Billy sat back in his lounge chair, put on the telly to keep an eye on the scores and relaxed. Within 30 minutes he had five out of six games showing green. At half-time, all six games were showing green and Billy was feeling very pleased with himself. He sent a text to Eddie and Martin to check that they had put on the same bet. Within minutes, they both replied positively thanking Billy for the tip-off and promising him a pint the next time they all went out together. With only 15 minutes left to play and all six teams showing green, the earlier ones having already finished, Billy sent a text to McGrath, Martin and Eddie advising to cash out now. Within minutes he had received a response from Martin and Eddie, both celebrating their victories. He thought it very unusual that McGrath had not responded right away and decided to call him. There was no response and the call went to voicemail.

Chapter Thirty Nine

Claire and Brian arrived at McGrath's home and immediately noticed that both his vehicles were parked in the driveway.

"Looks like he's at home then," said Brian getting out of the car.

A squad car with two uniformed officers pulled up behind the unmarked car. Brian had made sure he had backup, given McGrath's violent reputation. Claire approached the front door and rang the doorbell. There was no answer. She rang the bell again. Nothing.

"Brian, go round the back and check if you can see any sign of movement," Claire instructed.

"You two…" she said to the two PCs. "Go and check the front of the house." The two officers immediately did as they were told.

While she was waiting Claire took out her phone, looked up Rock Taxis and called the taxi office.

"Hello, Rock Taxis, how can I help you?" said the female voice on the other end of the call. Claire recognised it to be the older of the two operators.

"Hi, it's DI Redding from Dumbarton CID, is Mr McGrath in the office today?"

"No, I'm sorry. I haven't seen him all day. Is there anything wrong? I can call his mobile number if you need…"

"No, that won't be necessary. Thank you," said Claire and hung up the phone, just in time to spot Brian returning.

"He's not hiding in the back of the house," he said.

"The other two are checking the front of the house but I've got the horrible feeling that he's not in there. And I've just called his office and he's not there either."

The two PCs returned to the front door and confirmed that it was all clear.

"So, what do you think? Has McGrath done a runner?" asked Brian.

"Maybe," said Claire. "But why would he leave both cars in the driveway? It just doesn't add up."

It was only then that a thought occurred to her. Billy had said he had put another bet on this Saturday so surely McGrath would have been in contact with Billy. She took out her phone and made the call.

Billy was in his kitchen helping Maureen put the weekly shopping away when his phone rang. He immediately thought it was McGrath getting back to him and left the room to take the call in private.

"Hello," said Billy.

"Hello Billy, sorry to bother you but have you been in contact with McGrath today? You said you were putting on a bet and…"

"That's right. I sent him a text and left a message on his phone but got no reply. Why do you need to know?"

"Sorry Billy, I can't share that with you but if you do hear from him, can you let me know right away? It's important."

"Okay, but…"

"Thanks Billy," said Claire and ended the call. She looked at Brian and shook her head. "No contact."

"We should search the house. See if there are any clues as to where he might have gone," said Brian. He looked at the two officers. "Get the hammer."

"Hold on," said Claire who turned back towards the door and turned the handle. The door swung open.

"How the hell did you know that it was opened?" Brian asked.

"I didn't. It was just a hunch. Okay, let's search the house and get an all-points alert out for McGrath. Something is not right about this."

Chapter Forty

McGrath was sitting in the back seat of Digger's car alongside Bull. Bull was so big that he almost took up two of the three backseats which meant that McGrath was squeezed tight against the door. He knew that he was being taken to Petrie; he didn't know where and didn't know why but assumed it was to do with his handing over the business.

The car turned off the motorway at the Hillington junction, continued down towards the river and then out towards an old industrial estate which appeared to be full of rows and rows of abandoned warehouses.

Digger pulled the car into a parking bay in front of one of the warehouses and immediately spotted a black Mercedes a few spaces along. McGrath knew it had to belong to Petrie. Digger got out of the vehicle first and opened the backdoor which had the child lock switched on to prevent McGrath from escaping.

McGrath got out of the car and stretched his arms and upper body. He was closely followed by

Bull who struggled to move across the seat and slide out due to his sheer size. Digger approached the rusting metal door in the centre of the large structure and rang the bell. The door moaned as it was opened, screeching on the old hinges which had not been oiled for some time.

Petrie stood at the open doorway and stared at McGrath, who stared back, unsure what to say at this point. Petrie turned and went back inside the warehouse without saying a word. Bull gave McGrath a gentle push and he almost tripped head-first into the doorway but managed to catch his balance just in time and stood upright. As he looked around, he could tell the building had not been used for some time. The old brick walls glistened with dampness and were covered in some form of green fungus which was creeping upwards from every corner of the dank building. The lighting was very poor and although the overhead lights were turned on, only a few were working which created an array of eerie shadows throughout the cavernous space.

McGrath followed Digger into the middle of the old warehouse where Petrie was standing waiting for him. There were two tall circular brick pillars in the centre of the building, each about a metre in diameter reaching all the way up to the roof providing support for the large wooden beams and the rusting corrugated metal sheets which made up the roof.

"Tie him up," ordered Petrie.

Bull grabbed McGrath and pushed him against one of the brick pillars. He picked up the rope, which had been left lying on the ground in preparation for this meeting and tied McGrath's hands behind his back.

"Hey, what the fuck's going on? I thought we had a deal," said McGrath struggling to get free. Unfortunately, Bull was just too strong for him.

Petrie laughed and then sneered at McGrath. "A deal! Are you fucking taking the piss? You've got the fucking polis crawling all over you and you want me to do a deal."

"What do you mean, they've got nothing on..."

McGrath did not see it coming. Petrie swung an almighty blow which caught him on the left side of his cheek, his mouth exploded and at least two of his teeth flew out spraying blood everywhere. McGrath fell sideways onto the hard floor, his right shoulder taking the brunt of the fall. He was raging now, his earlier fear taken over by his anger but he was helpless to do anything about it. Bull picked him up and pushed him hard against the brick pillar.

"Let's start again, shall we?" snarled Petrie. "I know the local polis are all over you. What's her name again? Oh aye, I remember now, DI Redding. She found traces of drugs in the boot of your car. My fucking drugs... in your fucking car," he spat out, hardly able to contain his rage.

The look on McGrath's face was enough to tell Petrie that he didn't know anything about this. The anger had gone now and McGrath realised why he was here. He was going to die.

McGrath spat some more blood from his mouth and managed to mutter a response. "But they didn't arrest me, why didn't they arrest me?"

"Because, fuck wit, they're no' just after you, are they? They want me. They sent the drugs to the lab for analysis so they can trace them back to source."

McGrath was confused. "How can you possibly know all this, unless…"

The second blow hit him hard in the gut and McGrath folded over, winded and in agony.

Petrie allowed him some time to recover before continuing. "So, what I really need to know right now is - what the fuck are you up to McGrath? Offering me your business when you knew that the polis were after you. Are you so stupid to believe that they would just let you walk away? Was that it? Or were you planning on grassing me up at some point to secure your own freedom?"

"No, I would never grass anyone up, let alone you. I'd rather do the time. I've done it before and could do it again. You know that about me," McGrath pleaded.

Petrie had to admit to himself that McGrath had a point. "Well, what then? What possible motive could you have to hand over your business to me, *and for nothing*? You see, that's the bit that I just don't get." Petrie looked at Digger, who nodded in agreement.

McGrath suddenly realised that he had to tell Petrie the real reason why he no longer needed the drug money. "Okay, I'll tell you everything but you must promise to let me go after this is all over. I'll go to the police; I'll admit to dealing drugs but I'll never mention your name. I promise. But you must promise to let me go or you'll never find out the truth."

It was a brave move by McGrath. He knew that he had to offer something or he was a dead man.

Petrie stopped to think about it and then made up his mind. "Naw, where's the fun in that? Bull, let's persuade Mr McGrath here to spill his guts and if he's lucky I might let him live… keep him alive for now, understood? I want to hear what he has to say."

Bull nodded and started beating the living daylights out of McGrath, only stopping to pick him up when he fell to the ground. After a few minutes of being beaten up like a burst punching bag, McGrath's fighting spirit finally caved in. His face was a bloodied mess; one eye was completely swollen over, and his vision in the other one was severely impaired by the blood running from a cut just above the eye.

"Alright," he shouted. "I'll tell you; I'll fucking tell you everything, just keep this fucking ape away from me."

Petrie signalled to Bull to withdraw. "Okay then, let's hear it and it better be good."

McGrath told Petrie all about Billy's betting system and his plan to make enough money from the bookies to give up dealing drugs.

"Are you fucking kidding me? Do you seriously expect me to believe that you have a found system to beat the bookies?"

McGrath just nodded. He had nothing more to give and nothing more to lose. "Not me, a guy called Billy Taylor. He's some sort of mathematical genius; he worked it all out, but there's more than just the system he uses, he also seems to have a knack for picking the right teams which was why I did a deal with him. Don't ask me how, but it works. I've already made a lot of money on it and hopefully have won even more today."

McGrath had said enough to catch Petrie's attention. "So where is this, Billy Taylor? I want to speak to him face to face."

McGrath relaxed a little. "He lives somewhere in Dumbarton but I don't know where exactly... but Mick and Pat will know. I can call them and get them to bring Billy here to you. Billy's the key to all this and can verify everything I've said." He was lying of course; he knew where Taylor lived but his only chance of surviving this mess was if somehow Mick and Pat could read the room and take out Bull and Digger. Hopefully, Pat would come armed with his pistol.

Petrie pondered the proposal. He knew if he did get rid of McGrath he would also need to deal with Mick and Pat as they knew too much and inevitably would be the next targets for the police if McGrath suddenly disappeared.

"Okay, let's do that. Let's get them all in here," said Petrie, smiling to himself. He would soon have all the loose ends tied up!

Chapter Forty One

Claire was on her way home. She had left Brian in the station to co-ordinate the search for McGrath. He was under strict instructions to call her if McGrath was spotted. As she turned left onto the A82, her mobile phone rang. She grabbed the phone from her bag on the passenger seat and looked at the screen. It was Mulholland. She suddenly realised that she had forgotten to update him on progress with McGrath. "Shit!" she said out loud, reprimanding herself for being so forgetful. She pulled the car into the bus stop on her left and swiped the screen to accept the call. "Hello Sir, I was just about to call you about McGrath. He's..."

Mulholland interrupted her. "Disappeared? Yes, I know, I saw the alert and that's why I'm calling. My team were carrying out surveillance on one of our persons of interest in Glasgow and we may have spotted McGrath going to meet him."

"That's great news. Whereabouts? I'll get a team..."

"In an old warehouse, just outside Hillington, but there's no need for your team to get involved. I've got a team ready to go, but I thought you might want to be there when we take them down."

"Yes, but why me?" she asked.

Mulholland had anticipated the question. "Because DI Redding, you are fully up to speed with the charges against McGrath and therefore it would be very helpful for me to have you sit in on the interview, once we get him into custody."

Claire could not hide the delight in her voice. "Of course, Sir. What's the address and I'll head right there."

"I'll text it to you - it's an old industrial estate, south of the Hillington exit on the M8."

Claire looked at her watch. "That's great, Sir. I'll be there in about 20 minutes." Claire ended the call and immediately called DS O'Neill. "Hi Brian, we've got a sighting on McGrath."

"Really? Whereabouts?" Brian asked excitedly.

"He was seen entering a warehouse in Hillington. I'll send you the location. The Organised Crime Team were watching it and clocked McGrath going in. With any luck, he's meeting with his supplier and we'll bring the whole ring down."

"That's a relief, I thought he was gone for good."

"Yes, me too, anyway, I'm making my way there now. Can you get a hold of Jim and Paul and get them to bring in Mick Conroy and Pat Malloy for questioning? If we do manage to get McGrath, we wouldn't want them to find out and make a run for it."

"Okay, I'll see if I can get a hold of them. They're not going to be very happy though; it's their day off."

Claire considered this briefly and responded. "I know but this is what they have been working on for the last three weeks so they might prefer to be in on the action instead of hearing about it on Monday. Besides, they know all about Mick and Pat; where they live, the cars they drive, the pubs they drink in and so on. But if you can't get a hold of them, go ahead and ask DI McBride to identify a couple from his team to assist."

"Will do boss. Oh, who are you dealing with in the Organised Crime Team? Just in case I need to get in touch."

"Ask for Detective Superintendent Mulholland," she replied. "Have you heard of him?"

"You're kidding - not old Dutch? Yes, I've met him. It was a while ago right enough, a real nice guy and a bloody good cop. Say hello from me."

"Will do Brian. Let me know when you get Conroy and Malloy into custody. I'll be a lot happier knowing we've got them all under lock and key."

"Don't worry boss. We'll get them. You just concentrate on McGrath."

Chapter Forty Two

Mick and Pat pulled into Barnhill and headed up the steep incline where they hoped they would find Billy Taylor at home. McGrath sounded a bit rattled when he called Mick go get Billy. He also did not explain why he needed to see Taylor so urgently or why he was in a warehouse in Hillington but they knew better than to argue with him.

Mick parked the car on the main road at the foot of Barnhill Road and then he and Pat made their way up the path to Billy's house. Billy was the first to respond to the bell and opened the door. As soon as he recognised who it was, he stepped outside, closing the door behind him. "What the hell do you two want? This was not part of the deal with McGrath."

Mick ignored Billy's outburst. "McGrath wants to see you right away."

"What? Why? Why didn't he just call me? I've been trying to get a hold of him, even left a message on his phone!"

"Don't know," said Mick. "All I know is that he wants to see you right away, so come on."

Billy contemplated what to do next. He knew it couldn't be about the bet - or could it? McGrath would have doubled his money if he had cashed out on time. *Surely, he got my message!* Billy found himself getting agitated. "Okay, let me get my jacket. I'll need to tell Maureen that I'm going out."

Mick nodded and Billy turned and went back into the house. He grabbed his jacket and popped his head into the living room, where Maureen was sitting watching TV.

"I'm just nipping out for a wee while, be back soon." He didn't wait for a response, he turned and headed out the door anxious to find out what was going on.

It took a few seconds for Maureen to register what Billy had just said. She got to her feet and went to the window and saw Billy heading down Barnhill Road accompanied by two men. Something didn't look right about them. She considered calling the police but what could she say? *I'm worried because my husband has gone out with two strangers*. She decided to do nothing.

Chapter Forty Three

Claire followed the directions given by her phone and turned left into the industrial estate. It had started to rain heavily and her wipers barely cleared the water from the windscreen. The streetlights in the industrial estate were poor and struggled to light the road in front of her. She put on her full beam which helped and continued down the dark road, which had woodlands on one side and rows of old buildings on the other. She slowed down when she spotted a car parked about one hundred yards ahead, on the right side of the road. The driver of the parked vehicle immediately got out and waved to her. She pulled up beside the man, who was wearing a long dark Mackintosh coat with the collar turned up to protect his face - clearly prepared for the weather. She lowered her window so she could speak to him.

"Di Redding?" he asked.

"Yes, Superintendent Mulholland?"

He nodded. "Park your car beside mine. The warehouse is just up ahead."

She did as she was told and got out of the car.

"Follow me," he said and jogged to the side of the warehouse, which she noted had two cars parked outside the front.

"Where is your team?" she asked.

"Around the other side waiting for my instructions. I'll call them now," he said putting his right hand inside his coat pocket to get his phone but instead he produced a pistol. "Face the wall and put your hands behind your back detective."

Claire was in complete shock and did as instructed. The man took out a pair of handcuffs and cuffed her hands. He grabbed the back of Claire's jacket and pushed her around the corner of the building towards the doorway. Claire noticed a very smart looking Mercedes Benz parked just outside the doorway and quickly tried to memorise the number plate.

They stopped at the door of the warehouse. Mulholland, still holding the pistol in one hand, rang the bell with the other and within seconds the door opened to reveal the biggest man DI Redding had ever seen. He must have been at least six foot seven inches tall and four feet wide across the shoulders. Bull stood aside to let the detective enter the building. She heard the door close behind her and turned without thinking. Mulholland had disappeared and had left her with the man mountain. She looked ahead into the warehouse and could see McGrath and two other men.

McGrath had been badly beaten and she knew then that she was in serious trouble.

Chapter Forty Four

Claire had been right about Jim and Paul. Both men were delighted to hear that McGrath had been found and they were more than happy to help bring in Conroy and Malloy. The only fly in the ointment was that they failed to find either of them. They tried their homes, the office and their regular pubs but had turned up empty-handed.

The two officers sat in their car outside the taxi office, trying to think where else they might be. Jim decided it was time to call Brian.

"Hi Sarge, we've looked everywhere and can't find them. Conroy's car is not parked at his home. Do you think they've done a runner?"

"Maybe, but I don't get it. How could they possibly know that we were onto McGrath?"

"I've no idea, Sarge. But that's the way it looks. What do you want us to do?" asked Jim.

"Come back to the station. I'll contact the boss and let her know. At least we have McGrath."

Digger was the first to react when he saw DI Redding for the first time. "Well, well, what do we have here?" Aren't you a pretty wee thing?" He stood directly in front of her and gently lifted her chin so he could see her full face.

Claire smiled at Digger and before he could react, she kneed him in the groin. The sudden explosion of pain disabled him; he instinctively bent over, both hands holding his damaged groin which allowed Claire to take one step back and kick him in the face. Blood splattered from his mouth and he fell over onto the ground. It didn't take him long to recover though. He stood up, lunged at Claire, grabbed her throat and began to squeeze as hard as he could.

"Digger," growled Petrie. "Not now, you can have your fun later."

Digger did as he was told and stepped back, cursing under his breath. Petrie turned his attention to the young detective.

"You must be Detective Inspector Redding," said Petrie, who was rather amused by her fighting spirit.

"Yes, and you are?" she hissed back.

"Petrie. Not that it matters, who I am. You'll not live to tell anyone about this little gathering."

It was Digger's turn to start grinning. "Just say the word boss and I'll take care of the little bitch."

Petrie raised his hand to indicate that Digger should stop talking. "They'll be plenty of time for that later but for now I need to know how much she knows about my business and how much this piece of shite has told them," growled Petrie, looking over at McGrath.

Claire said nothing. She had no idea what was going on and had decided to say as little as possible. She still found it hard to believe that Mulholland would turn her over to Petrie. Brian had said he was a good cop so it just didn't make any sense - unless Petrie had something on him to use as blackmail.

"So detective, how much do you know about my business?" asked Petrie.

Claire looked up at Petrie. "Nothing, we were after McGrath."

Petrie walked slowly around Claire, his eyes fixed on hers, like a wolf stalking its prey. "Nothing? So why didn't you arrest him? After all, you found traces of drugs in the boot of his car?"

Claire could not hide her surprise at that little revelation. "What? How could you know about that?"

She didn't see the blow coming. Petrie hit her across the face with the back of his right hand, her top lip burst open and she felt a crack as the bridge of her nose snapped. She staggered to the side just managing to stay on her feet. She steadied herself and glared at Petrie. Suddenly, the penny dropped.

"Mulholland, he's been feeding you everything. That's how you know about the traces of drugs and that's how McGrath knew to hide everything before we raided his house. Is that why you beat him up?

Because he was careless. Because his drugs could be linked to your supply and …"

She was interrupted by the ring tone of her mobile phone. Petrie immediately grabbed her, searched her coat pockets and removed the offending phone. He looked at the screen. "Who's Brian? Your boyfriend? Or perhaps another one of your shitty polis pals?" He laughed and threw the phone at the ground. The screen smashed but the phone continued to ring, before stopping abruptly when Petrie smashed his heel onto the phone and scraped it along the hard surface of the concrete floor.

Claire stared down at her smashed phone, wishing she had the foresight to put it on silent but it was too late now and the only means of her current location being traced had gone. She hoped Brian had received her text with her location, but right now - she was on her own and helpless. Her line of thought was suddenly interrupted by the ring of the doorbell. This caught everyone by surprise.

Petrie immediately went over to Digger and whispered some instructions. Digger nodded and went to the door with Bull. Digger withdrew the pistol which he had hidden in the waistline of his jeans and approached the door quietly. He slid the metal flap which was at eye level and peered into the darkness. He relaxed when he saw Mick and Pat with another man, who he assumed must be Billy Taylor. He stood aside, pistol still in his hand, and signalled to Bull to open the door.

The three men entered the old building but stopped when they realised that McGrath and DI Redding had been beaten up. Mick was the first to react. "What the fuck is going on?"

Pat reached for his gun and was about to draw it when the first gunshot was fired. Mick flinched not understanding what was happening and then Pat hit the ground. The bullet had entered his back and went straight into his heart tearing and shredding the soft tissue before coming to a halt in his sternum. Death was instant. Mick froze with fear and immediately put his hands in the air. Billy, who was standing next to Pat panicked and threw himself onto the ground putting both hands over his ears; his ear drums battered by the sound of the gunshot. Digger casually walked over to Mick, pointed the gun to the back of his head and blew his brains out. The front of Mick's face exploded outwards as the force of the flattened bullet escaped via the front of his skull.

Billy couldn't move; he was paralyzed with the shock at the sudden outburst of violence.

McGrath, who was initially pleased to see Billy enter the building, was also in shock and was now terrified; his physical demeanour now betraying his earlier bravado. He was a broken man.

Claire, after the initial shock, was now taking in the whole scene and desperately trying to find a way out but it seemed hopeless. She scanned the building and could see another door at the back of the vast hall but it was too far away. She would never make it. It was bad enough that she had put herself in danger but now that Billy, an innocent, had been introduced into the mix, the situation had changed for the worse. She just hoped that Billy had enough sense not to acknowledge her; pretend that he didn't know her. If Petrie knew that Billy was assisting her with the investigation then the next bullet would inevitably go his way.

Bull picked Billy up off the ground and pushed him towards Petrie. Billy stared at McGrath's damaged face and almost threw up. His stomach was doing cartwheels.

"So, you are Billy Taylor, the genius who has come up with the system to beat the bookies," said Petrie, not really asking a question but seeking a response all the same.

Billy looked at McGrath who was nodding, his eyes pleading with Billy to tell Petrie everything, to reassure him that McGrath's motive was genuine and therefore he had been truthful. Billy took a breath - he was physically shaking. "Well, it's just a set of rules which reduces the risk of losing," he mumbled.

Petrie was not entirely convinced by Billy's rather weak response to his question and quickly followed it up with another. "But you've made a lot of money for McGrath? Yes?"

"Yes, we, eh, have a d…d…deal," stuttered Billy.

"Yes, McGrath did mention a deal. Tell me about it," asked Petrie.

Billy turned to McGrath looking for some assurance. Again, McGrath nodded, confirming that Billy should proceed. "Well, I… em… eh, provide the teams to bet on, and he… eh, McGrath, provides the stake. And, eh… in return, he gives me 25%," said Billy, who was now really struggling to hold himself together.

"Fucking 25%? Are you kidding me? He takes all the risk and you walk away with 25%. What sort of fucking deal is that?"

Billy didn't know how to respond to that particular question, so he just nodded and remained silent. Petrie answered the question for him. "I'll tell you what sort of deal that is, it's fucking shite. Well, Billy, here's my deal. You're going to put a bet on for me and if you lose you are fucking dead. How's that for a deal?"

"What? No, my deal's with McGrath." As soon as Billy uttered the words, he regretted it.

"Digger," Petrie commanded.

Digger raised the pistol and shot McGrath in the chest. McGrath gargled desperately trying to fill his damaged lungs with air. If the first shot missed the heart, the second didn't and McGrath slumped to the ground on his knees and then fell forward onto his broken face.

"What was that you were saying about a deal?" asked Petrie.

Billy's eyes filled with tears; his nerves now completely shattered.

"Aw for fuck's sake! Wipe away those bloody tears. What sort of fucking wimp are you?"

Billy used the sleeve of his jacket to wipe the tears away and looked up at Petrie.

"Right Billy, you and I are taking a wee ride. Bull. Tie him up and put him in my car. I'll be out in a minute." He turned towards Claire who was still trying to think of a way out of this mess but had nothing. She was relieved that Billy had not given their secret away and that Petrie had a use for him. That would keep him alive for a little bit longer. All he had to do was keep on providing winning bets and he would be fine.

"So detective, it seems that it's time for us to say goodbye. Digger, you can have your fun now but when you're finished, I want this place cleaned up. No evidence, understood?"

"No problem, boss. I know what to do."

Petrie nodded and marched towards the exit and left the building.

Bull came back inside and closed the door behind him. He smiled to himself. It wasn't just going to be Digger who had fun with the pretty little detective. He had his own plans for her.

Digger stood opposite Claire, carefully assessing the best way to get what he wanted. "So detective, are you going to cooperate or are we going to do this the hard way."

"What do you think?" said Claire, who had decided she had no option but to fight for her life.

Digger was more cautious this time and did not approach the detective who was clearly looking for another opportunity to kick him in the balls. He circled her and then stopped, removed the gun and placed it on the ground. "Wouldn't want any unfortunate accidents, would we?" he said grinning.

Claire closed her eyes as the unthinkable was about to happen. Exhausted from the exertion of trying to resist, she knew she was about to be raped; one of the many terrible things that she had prayed would never happen to her. Tears began to fill her eyes as she felt Digger's rough hands push up her long skirt, searching for her underwear, grabbing and then ripping the flimsy material away.

Suddenly, there was a loud bang and then another as the metal door gave way to the hammer used by officers from the Armed Response Team, who rushed into the building, followed by DS O'Neill and DC Black.

"Armed Police. Put your hands on your head," they shouted. "Armed Police!" they repeated again and again. They were equipped with standard automatic rifles, which only trained firearms officers were permitted to use.

At first Claire was just as confused as Digger and Bull but she soon realised what was going on and the relief was euphoric.

Chapter Forty Five

Digger scrambled along the ground, his bare arse and genitalia visible for all to see. He quickly found the pistol where he had left it and slipped behind the pillar where McGrath was lying face down in the dirt. He gathered himself, stood up with his back to the pillar and quickly pulled his jeans up. He took a few breaths, turned, and fired a single round in the direction of the nearest police officer, grazing his shoulder. The injured officer dived to the ground while the other officers took cover and started firing back. Several shots ricocheted off the pillar, which protected Digger from their aim. Bull took the opportunity to run towards the backdoor of the building which he hit at full speed, side on. The rusting hinges and lock easily disintegrated with his weight and momentum. Once outside, he glanced left and right seeking the best route to escape and decided to run to the left. Paul decided to go after him and headed back out of the front entrance to avoid the gunfire. He sprinted round the side of the building at top speed; his boxing training paying off. Jim, who had been keeping guard outside the door, joined the pursuit but could not match Paul's speed and quickly fell behind his athletic colleague.

Inside the building, Brian had managed to crawl around the perimeter towards Claire who was lying still on the ground. He was trying hard to put aside the scene he had witnessed when they first burst into the building: the two men pinning her to the ground, one with his trousers down which meant only one thing.

Brian crawled towards Claire, praying that she was alright. "Claire," he whispered. "Claire, it's Brian."

Claire heard Brian's voice, turned her body towards him and whispered back. "Five shots. One left." Brian instantly understood what Claire wanted him to do. She knew that the type of revolver which Digger was using only held six bullets, so one more and he would need to reload which would give Brian a chance to take him down. Brian lay motionless beside Claire waiting for his opportunity.

Digger was getting desperate. The backdoor, which was now a gaping hole, looked like his only means of escape. He also knew that he had one bullet left. This was it, his only chance. He took a long breath, turned and fired off a shot at another of the armed police officers and ran as fast as he could towards the back door, zigzagging across the floor to avoid the retaliatory bullets which inevitably would come his way. Brian made his move and tried to intercept Digger but to Brian's horror Digger saw him coming. He turned and pointed the gun directly at Brian. A rally of shots could be heard as Digger fell to the ground.

"Ceasefire, ceasefire" Brian shouted as loudly as he could, but it was too late. By the time he reached Digger, he was dead.

Bull was beginning to run out of steam - he wasn't built to run and could hear the officer chasing him getting closer and closer. Eventually he stopped and turned to face his opponent who was still running but luckily did not appear to be armed.

Paul slowed when he saw that the big man had stopped and raised his fists preparing to fight. Bull smiled. He was confident that he would get the better of the policeman who was at least five stone lighter than he was and considerably shorter. Paul started to dance around Bull, bobbing and weaving as he had been trained to do. Bull took a swing at him and missed. Paul's reaction speed was far superior to the heavy muscle bound monster he was facing. Paul started jabbing at Bull with his left fist again and again, the blows irritating the big man but having no real impact.

Paul ducked to the left and launched a right hook which caught the beast of a man full on the jaw. Bull staggered but remained on his feet. Paul hit him again and again but Bull stood tall and decided enough was enough. He charged at Paul, both arms open, grabbing Paul's upper body, wrestling him to the ground and landing on top of him in one clumsy movement. Bull sat up and grabbed Paul's neck with both hands and started to squeeze the life out of him.

Jim, gasping for breath, finally caught up with his colleague and looked in horror as he saw Bull sitting on top of Paul, strangling him. He knew he was too weak to take on Bull by himself but had to act quickly. He scanned the area for anything that he could use as a weapon and found an old brick. Then, with all his strength he smashed the brick against the back of Bull's head. Bull flinched and then collapsed, unconscious, on top of Paul.

Chapter Forty Six

Brian was sitting beside Claire looking around at the carnage that surrounded them. After a few minutes of swearing and cursing, he eventually managed to pick the lock on her handcuffs using a small bent nail he'd found lying on the floor. As soon as she was free from the cuffs, Claire massaged her sore arms and wrists, trying to help the stiff muscle tissue to return to normal.

"How did you know, Brian? I mean, know that I was in trouble?"

Brian did his best to explain. "Well, firstly, I tried to call your mobile to let you know that we couldn't find Conroy or Malloy." He looked over at their two bodies. "And now I know why."

"Yes, that's when Petrie heard my phone ring and smashed it to pieces but... how did you know that I was in trouble?" she asked again.

"So, when it was clear that I couldn't get a hold of you on your phone, I decided to call the Organised

Crime Team, to ask them to get a message to you. But when I asked to speak to Mulholland, they said he was off duty which started to ring alarm bells in my head. And when I told them that they must be mistaken as he was involved in the Hillington Operation with you, they said they didn't know about any operation. I knew then that something was wrong and arranged for the armed response team to meet us at the warehouse and the rest, as they say, is history."

"Well, all I can say is thank the Lord you made that call Brian. They were going to kill me... after they had finished with me."

"Sorry to ask but did they... rape you?" Brian asked sheepishly.

"No, but a few minutes more and they would have," said Claire, playing down the situation. There was no way she could have explained what she had just gone through to Brian without crumbling into a complete mess.

"Thank God for that," said Brian, clearly relieved but also sensing that she didn't want to talk about it.

Claire nodded, then paused for a moment to compose herself. "So, if the Organised Crime Team knew nothing about the operation, who in the name of hell was I dealing with, if not Mulholland?"

"That's what I would like to know," said the man approaching them. He was six foot three, had thin grey hair and wore a long green coat, which was drenched in rain.

Brian looked up and immediately got to his feet.

"Hello, Brian, long time no see."

"Hello Dutch, sorry, I mean Sir."

"Paul… Paul, come on mate, wake up!" shouted Jim. He put his ear to Paul's mouth to check if he was breathing. Nothing! "Shit, shit, shit!" He tilted Paul's head back slightly to open the airway, pinched his nose and blew twice into his lungs. Jim then started to do chest compressions the way he had been taught in basic training. "One, two, three, four…" He reached the count of fifteen and suddenly Paul gasped for air, inhaling deeply and filling his lungs.

"Paul, Paul mate, can you hear me? It's Jim."

Paul opened his eyes and coughed. He gasped for some air and finally said, "What happened?"

"I had to give you the fucking kiss of life, mate. That's what happened," said Jim, who promptly wiped his lips in disgust.

"Well, I hope you don't have fucking COVID," Paul replied smiling at Jim. "I've no' had my booster yet."

Jim laughed. "Okay you stay there. I'm going to check on this big bastard." He shuffled over to Bull and could see from the heaving of his chest that he was still alive. At first, he thought the blow had killed him, but not Bull; it would take much more than that to finish him off Jim quickly cuffed Bull and when he was confident that he was securely manacled, called an ambulance.

"You must be DI Redding," said Mulholland quickly turning his attention to Claire.

"Yes, Sir," said Claire, quickly fixing her skirt and blouse, before standing up to address the senior officer.

"Are you alright? That nose looks pretty bad?" he said, gesturing to her face.

Claire instinctively touched her nose and winced at the pain. "It only hurts when I touch it."

"So, I see," he said smiling. "Look, I'm sorry to have to ask but did you get a good look at the man who pretended to be me?"

"Yes, I did Sir. He's in his late forties, about five feet ten, has dark brown hair, blue eyes..."

Mulholland nodded. "Is this him?" He showed Claire a photo image of a man on his phone.

"Yes, that's him," she confirmed.

Mulholland's face dropped. "He's DCI Craig Jardine with the Organised Crime Team. Well, I better put out a call for him to be brought in A.S.A.P."

It was clear from his face that Mulholland was gutted to hear that one of his men was involved with Petrie and worse than that, had deliberately put another officer at risk.

"I take it you thought it was him from the outset, Sir?"

"What makes you say that Inspector?"

"You had his picture ready to show me."

"Of course, you don't miss much, do you?" he said and turned to go.

"Wait Sir, what about Petrie?"

Mulholland stopped dead on the spot. "Petrie?"

"Yes, Sir, it was Petrie who broke my nose and ordered the killings."

"Petrie? He was here? You witnessed this?" Mulholland's mood lightened.

"Yes Sir. I did and so did Billy Taylor?"

"Who is Billy Taylor?"

"He a civilian who was helping us gather information on McGrath and... somehow... well he ended up here."

"So where is he now?" Mulholland asked.

"Petrie took him. I'm pretty sure he's driving a black Mercedes Benz, number plate BP67..." She paused. "Shit, what was it again?" Her mind had gone completely blank. She closed her eyes and tried to visualise the plate.

"Got it, BP67 TSR," said Claire pleased with herself.

"Right," said Mulholland snapping into action. I'll get my team to check to see if we get at a hit on any of the ANPR cameras. He's bound to use the M8 if he's heading back into the city."

Just at that moment Brian's mobile phone rang. He looked down at the small screen. "It's Jim," he said to Claire.

"Hi Jim, what's the situation?" asked Brian.

Jim briefly explained what had happened to Paul and confirmed that they had Bull in custody.

"And Paul's going to be okay?" asked Brian.

"Yes, he'll be fine. He's with the paramedic now."

"That's great Jim, well done," said Brian.

Claire was staring at him expectantly. "Well, what happened?"

"They got the big fella. Paul got hurt in the process, nearly died in fact. Jim had to give him CPR but he's fine now."

"That'll be Thomas Davidson, also known as Bull," said Mulholland.

"Hold on," said Claire. "How did Jim manage to take him down on his own, he's huge?"

"Apparently he hit him with a brick," said Brian smiling to himself, and for the first time that evening Claire also managed a smile.

Chapter Forty Seven

Petrie had travelled on the M8 to make his way back to the pub. It was the quickest route and although he knew all about the Automated Number Plate Recognition System, he had no reason to suspect the police were looking for his car. The journey had only taken fifteen minutes - they had missed the rush hour traffic and there were no games on at Parkhead that Saturday so traffic had been lighter than usual.

Petrie parked his car at the back of the pub, carefully navigating the narrow side street which led to the rear access. He stopped the car, looked around to see if anyone was around and then got out and opened the back door. Billy was lying on the floor of the car, jammed in between the front and back seats. His long legs were folded up over his chest and had been resting on the passenger door until Petrie opened it. Petrie grabbed Billy's jacket and pulled him up into a sitting position. "Right, let's get you out of there." He put Billy's feet on the ground and heaved him up and out of the car. Billy wobbled a bit as the blood returned to his feet and legs. He could feel the shooting pains of pins and needles as the blood made its way through the capillaries on the soles of his feet and then upwards towards his calf muscles, causing them to cramp.

Once out of the car, Billy stretched his legs and took in his surroundings. He could hear the noise coming from the rear entrance of the pub. "Where are we?" he asked.

Petrie ignored him and shoved Billy towards the back door of the public house. He opened the door and looked inside. Having confirmed that it was all clear he pushed Billy inside and then led him through a door on their left. Petrie closed the small door behind him and turned on the light.

Billy could see boxes of crisps and nuts, trays of soft drinks, and other pub supplies stacked up on shelves on one side of the storeroom.

Petrie went over to the door at the far side of the room, opened it and turned on the light.

"Okay, Billy. Down you go," said Petrie, who pointed down to the cellar stairs.

Billy did as he was told. He carefully stepped down the narrow staircase, reached the bottom and looked around. He spotted an old crate and sat down. He could see the beer casks and connecting hoses which fed the siphons upstairs in the pub. There were also several other casks, which were stacked in the corner of the cellar waiting to be connected whenever the others ran dry.

Petrie followed Billy down the stairs and untied the short piece of rope, which Bull had used to bind his wrists together. "Okay Billy, you'll need to stay in here until Digger and Bull get back and then we'll decide what to do with you. I'm going to trust you to behave yourself so no shouting or trying to escape. Understand?"

Billy nodded despondently.

"Good." Petrie turned, went up the stairs and closed the door. He slid the bolt across the door and used an old but solid looking padlock to secure it.

Chapter Forty Eight

After an hour of waiting anxiously, Maureen decided that she had to find out what on earth was going on. Billy had said he would be back soon but she had heard nothing since he had left with those two dodgy-looking characters. Her fears only worsened when he didn't respond to her calls. She would have been even more concerned if she knew that Billy's phone was ringing out on the floor of Petrie's car; it had fallen out of his jacket pocket when Bull had shoved him into the backseat.

She decided it was time to call the police. After a few minutes of explaining and then waiting on the switchboard operator to transfer the call to CID, Maureen was finally connected to DS O'Neill. She briefly explained her concerns to Brian, who was unsure how to respond without causing her further alarm. He couldn't tell her the truth - that her husband had been taken by one the most dangerous gangsters in Glasgow - so he decided to pretend that Billy's abduction was news to him.

"Thanks for letting us know Mrs Taylor. I'm sure Billy will be fine but just in case I'll send a couple of officers over to your house right away to take a full statement and we'll take it from there."

Maureen was pleasantly surprised that her concerns had been taken so seriously. "Thank you so much, Sergeant. It really isn't like Billy just to go off like that and those two men looked... well... like trouble. Thanks again."

"You're welcome... and don't worry, we'll find him," he said, meaning every word of it. Brian had every intention of sending officers to her home but he would make also sure that one of those officers was from family liaison, who would stay with Mrs Taylor. Just in case things went badly.

Brian made his way over to Claire and Mulholland. "That was Maureen Taylor reporting that Billy has gone missing. From the description given, it looks like Conroy and Malloy picked him up from his home and brought him here."

"You didn't tell her about Petrie?" asked Claire.

"No, I didn't think that would be wise but I did agree to get some officers over to her house to take a statement."

"Yes, we'll probably need her statement whatever happens tonight," said Claire.

"Right, so what's the plan?" asked Brian.

Mulholland spoke first. "We've just had confirmation that Petrie's car was picked up by ANPR on the M8 and is now parked behind his pub. We haven't got a lot of time to waste so we need to act now. I've got the Armed Response Team set to go to his pub but it's not going to be easy as the pub will be full of customers at this time of night."

"Yes, I can see how that could be tricky," said Claire.

Mulholland sighed. "I'm sorry Brian but I'm going to have to ask you to stay here and wait for the SOCO to arrive. Claire – you need to get yourself to a hospital and get that nose fixed."

"No Sir," she said indignantly. "That can wait. I want to go with you. After all, I'm the reason you have enough evidence to put Petrie away for life and I'm also responsible for Billy Taylor being involved in this, and besides... I have a plan to get everyone in the pub out safely and hopefully take Petrie alive."

Mulholland was impressed by her boldness and determination to put things right. "Okay then detective. Let's hear your plan."

Chapter Forty Nine

The police vehicles were parked in an abandoned plot of ground five hundred yards away from Petrie's pub. Mulholland, who was in the main control unit, was busy briefing the Armed Response Team on DI Redding's very simple but effective plan. "Now remember, we don't enter the building until it is cleared. Most people will leave through the front entrance but some might come out the back door so be prepared for that. Petrie's office is upstairs so I think he will come out the back way but I want eyes on both the front and backdoor to make sure we don't miss him. He might have some of his men with him but more importantly, he could also have a hostage, Billy Taylor, who we believe is being held captive somewhere in the pub. Remember, Petrie is dangerous and could be armed, so take no chances. Right. Any questions?"

No one responded.

"Okay DI Redding. You're on. Once all armed officers are in position, I'll give you the signal to go in. From now on, all communications are via the radio. Let's go."

Claire approached the back of the pub with caution and immediately notified Mulholland that she was ready to go. He confirmed that the Armed Response Team were in position and gave her the go-ahead to proceed. She carefully opened the back door and looked inside to see if anyone was there. To her relief, the back corridor was empty. She skipped inside and quickly found the ladies' toilets, which were just before the internal door leading to the main pub. She could hear the noise of the music and the loud chatter coming from inside the pub and could tell that it was busy.

She entered the ladies' toilets and could see that one of the cubicles was occupied. Thankfully the next thing she heard was the flush of the toilet and the door unlocking. Claire went to the sink and washed her hands and watched the young woman do the same at the sink opposite her cubicle. She waited until the woman left the room and took out the small smoke canister, which the Armed Response Team had provided. She looked up and could see the smoke detector on the ceiling in the centre of the room and smiled to herself. It was just as she had hoped. She pulled the pin on top of the canister and rolled it under the furthest away cubicle. The smoke immediately filled the room but much to Claire's dismay the smoke detector did not activate. "Shit!" she said out loud to herself. Thinking quickly, Claire opened the door to the corridor and used some hand wipes to keep it wedged open, thus allowing smoke to enter the back corridor. She made a quick decision, entered the pub, shouting "Fire, fire!" at the top of her voice.

At first, no one in the pub reacted but as soon as the smoke began to enter the room, there was mass panic and people started running in the opposite direction and out of the front door. Claire spotted the fire alarm switch on the wall next to the fire door, broke the glass with her elbow and pressed the button. The noise of the siren was excruciatingly loud. Claire hoped that this would bring Petrie running downstairs and out the back door, which was an integral part of her plan.

Confident that everyone inside the pub, including the bar staff, was heading to the front door, Claire went back through the door and closed it behind her. She headed straight for the backdoor as planned but stopped dead as she passed the storeroom on her right. She was sure she had heard shouting coming from the room and then she recognised the voice – it was Billy.

She burst into the small storeroom and found the light switch on the wall beside the door. The fire alarm inside the storeroom was ringing loudly. The shouting was coming from a door at the back of the room which was padlocked. She went up to the door and shouted to Billy. "Billy? Billy, it's DI

Redding. Stand back from the door and I'll try to kick it open."

She took a few steps back, ran and raised her right foot to stamp at the area near the padlock as hard as she could but the heavy door did not budge. She tried again and failed. Thinking quickly, she looked around. There were some empty beer barrels in the corner and she immediately went and lifted one with both hands. Even though it was clearly empty, the metal barrel was still heavier than she anticipated. She managed to lift it off the ground and walked slowly to the door. Just as she prepared to strike the padlock, she heard the door of the storeroom open and turned around.

Petrie was just as surprised to see the young detective, alive and well, as she was surprised to see him. He immediately put his hand into his jacket pocket and brought out a small pistol which he pointed at Claire and smiled. "I suppose you're the reason for the fire alarm and that wee smoke canister in the ladies' toilet?" he asked, not really expecting a response and none was offered.

"I have to say, detective. I'm impressed. I've no idea how you managed to escape Bull and Digger but I'd take my hat off to you - if I had one. Sadly, it looks like your luck has finally run out."

Claire's eyes suddenly shifted to the door behind Petrie and he instinctively turned to see what had drawn her intention. That was all she needed, a split second of distraction before she used all her strength to throw the heavy metal barrel at Petrie's upper body. The barrel hit its target but not before he reacted and fired a shot, which was heard by the Armed Support Team who were waiting outside the backdoor.

The call on the radio was almost instantaneous. "Shot fired, shot fired inside the pub."

Mulholland reacted immediately. "All units, enter the building with caution. Shot fired. Unarmed police officer inside the building. I repeat, police officer inside the building."

The shot just missed Claire and struck the door behind her. However, the flying barrel didn't miss its mark and caught Petrie in the face.

Claire didn't wait to see if he was hurt - she immediately ran, jumped and kicked him hard in the chest. Several his ribs cracked as the air in Petrie's lungs exploded out of his mouth from the sheer force of the kick. As he stooped down to gather in some much needed air, the young detective took advantage and booted him hard in the face, breaking his nose in the process. Petrie fell face forward to the ground stunned by the blow and before he could recover, Claire sat on Petrie's back and handcuffed him. She reached for her radio and was about to call it in when two armed officers burst in the room.

"It's okay," said Claire, who was still sitting on Petrie. "As you can see Petrie's been secured and I believe Billy Taylor's trapped in the cellar over there." She got up, bent over Petrie and started rifling through his pockets. "Ah, here they are," she said, holding up a set of keys which she passed to one of the officers. Petrie said nothing.

Chapter Fifty

Claire woke up the next morning in the comfort of her own bed but feeling rather nauseous. It was not that surprising given her latest trauma but something did not feel quite right. It had been a late night by the time she had fully briefed Mulholland on her fight with Petrie and then, as ordered, she had gone to the A&E for a full check-up. They had taken some blood as a precaution and advised that she would need plastic surgery on her nose, which they had temporarily reset until she could get an appointment with the plastic surgeon.

Peter had been shocked to see her return home with bruising on her face and a strapped-up nose but she soon had him laughing as she described how she had taken down one of the biggest gangsters in Scotland with an empty beer barrel. She failed to mention anything about the attempted rape or shooting and with the help of a couple of glasses of wine, she went to bed and drifted into a surprisingly deep and peaceful sleep.

However, now fully awake, the memories of the previous night's activities slowly returned to her as she sat bolt upright in the bed. As she relived the scene in the warehouse inside her head, she suddenly had the urge to vomit and ran to the bathroom, where she emptied the full contents of her stomach. *Shouldn't have had that second glass of wine!*

Peter, now awake with the sound of the retching, got out of bed and staggered through to the bathroom, still half asleep. Claire was kneeling on the floor, head over the toilet.

"Are you alright Claire?" he asked.

She glared up at him, her eyes responding on behalf of her stomach – *what do you think?*

After a minute of spitting and clearing her mouth, she decided that it was safe to move away from the toilet seat. She went over to the sink and took a sip of cold water and then brushed her teeth to remove the horrible acidic taste.

Peter stood there watching her, not entirely sure what to say next. Claire now had bloodshot eyes to add to her bruised face and broken nose. She finished cleaning her teeth and turned to Peter who was standing at the door. She read the concerned look on his face and smiled at him. "Sorry, I'm fine now. Must have been a reaction to last night's excitement and maybe the wine. Probably the wine. Remind me never to drink so late at night again... anyway, I'm fine now, honest. Off you go back to bed. I'll be through in a minute. I'll need to clean the toilet."

Peter deliberately did not look down to see the toilet seat. The smell was enough to turn his stomach. He went back to the bedroom and looked at the clock. It was just after eight and he knew it wouldn't be long before Sally would get restless and demand some attention. "Claire," he said. "I'm just popping downstairs to see to Sally. You go back to bed and I'll get you a nice cup of tea."

Claire knew there was little chance of her getting back to sleep but went back to bed and waited for her tea. She was still feeling a little bit queasy when she lay down so she sat up in the bed and picked up her mobile phone, turning it on. She could see there were two missed calls and two voice mails. One was from Brian but the other was a number she did not recognise. She listened to Brian's call first. She had felt sorry about leaving Brian to take charge of things in the warehouse but it was the only way Mulholland would have allowed her to go to Petrie's pub. Brian's message was very brief and to the point. Mulholland had been in touch to confirm that DCI Jardine had been arrested at Glasgow airport - trying to flee the country, and that Mulholland had instigated an internal investigation which would involve Claire giving evidence whenever she was fit to do so. Normally, the thought of providing evidence against a fellow officer would be unpleasant to say the least but, on this occasion, Claire was more than happy to assist. The second message was a call from the hospital. *That was quick. I wonder if they have managed to squeeze me in for surgery.* She called the number given in the message and spoke to one of the nurses.

"Hello, it's DI Redding. You left a message for me to call back."

"Yes, that's correct. Now let me just check. Ah, yes, here they are. Yes, we have the first set of results back on your blood tests. There's nothing to worry about but we just thought you should know that you're pregnant."

Claire was stunned into silence.

"Hello, are you still there?" the nurse asked.

"What? Yes, sorry I'm still here."

"I assume it's a bit of surprise but I hope a happy one?"

"What? Yes... yes, we were trying for a baby, I just didn't expect it... well... to be so soon. That's all."

"If I had a pound for every pregnant mother who..." the nurse said, before Claire rather abruptly cut her off.

"So, what happens next?" asked Claire, who suddenly realised that she was completely unprepared for this.

"Well, you should go and see your GP who will tell you all you need to know. I take it it's your first?"

"Yes," said Claire. "Yes, it is. Sorry, but I'm going to have to go." She threw the phone on her bed and ran to the toilet. Apparently, she hadn't emptied her whole stomach.

Peter was busy downstairs making breakfast for Sally and tea for Claire. He had let Sally out into the garden to relieve herself and now she was back in the kitchen looking to be fed. He put down the bowl and moved back to allow her to get stuck in. He started to wash his hands when the phone in the hall rang. Peter quickly wiped his hands with a paper towel and ran out to the hall and picked up the phone. "Hello," he said.

"Is DI Redding there?" asked the gruff voice on the other end of the line.

"Yes, she's upstairs, sleeping, I think. Can I take a message?" Peter assumed it was yet another early morning call from the station. Some of the duty sergeants sounded pretty rough, but this one took the biscuit.

"Aye, you can tell her if she testifies, she and everyone she cares about is dead." The line went dead and Peter froze with fear.

Claire, having recovered from another phase of retching, came down the stairs to the hallway, where Peter was standing in a daze, still holding the phone.

"Who was that?" she asked.

"What? Oh, eh, just some salesperson trying to sell timeshare," he replied hesitantly.

"Oh, right," she said. "Well don't look so miserable, come on into the kitchen and sit down. I've got some news which I guarantee will cheer you up."

Epilogue - Billy

Saturday had to be the worst day of my life. Firstly, there was that God-awful warehouse where McGrath and his men were shot. And if that experience was not terrifying enough, to be locked in that horrible cellar by Petrie, not knowing what was going to happen to me, not knowing if I would ever see Maureen again - that was the lowest point.

I've no idea how DI Redding managed to escape the warehouse, never mind take down Petrie but I will be forever grateful. *She must be the bravest person I've ever met.* I have never been more scared in my life than I was when I heard the gunshot outside the cellar door. I thought she had to be dead and that I was next in line. The surprise and relief that I felt when she opened the door was life-changing for me. I knew there and then that I was done with gambling and swore to myself that the first thing I would do was delete that bloody app. That is, if I ever get my phone back; the police found it in Petrie's car and took it away as evidence.

Needless to say, I spent hours on Saturday night giving a full statement to various police officers and then finally got home in the early hours of Sunday morning. Thankfully, the police had arranged for an officer to stay with Maureen until I returned and therefore, she knew that I was safe.

I didn't have the heart to tell her everything that happened last night but she's still very upset, and will be for some time, as you can imagine. I suppose she'll find out the whole truth eventually, when the case goes to trial but according to the police that could be a long way off. Apparently, the courts are way behind due to COVID!

I'm dreading that day, and if it wasn't for DI Redding... well, I'm not sure that I would be brave enough to testify against Petrie. But I owe her my life, so it's the least I can do. Anyway, I need to go now, the house phone is ringing. Who in their right mind calls at this time on a Sunday morning?

The end.

About this book

All characters named within the story are fictitious and any similarity to real people is coincidental.

Billy's set of rules are also a work of fiction so please do not think you can use them to beat the bookies – you won't.

After all, gambling is a mug's game!

Other titles by Andrew Hawthorne

There's no such thing as a Perfect Crime!
(DI Redding Book 1)

Claire Redding, a rising star within Police Scotland, is being fast tracked for greater things. Having played a key role in bringing down a major drugs gang in Glasgow, Claire is promoted to the position of Detective Inspector and transferred to 'L' Division in Dumbarton where she must convince a well-established team of detectives that she is as good as her reputation suggests. She is asked to solve a series of local burglaries which all have one thing in common - they all appear to be perfect crimes. DI Redding firmly believes that there is no such thing as a perfect crime and is determined to catch the elusive thief and further enhance her career prospects.

The pressure builds on the ambitious young DI when the burglaries are linked to a murder and local and national media ramp up interest in the case. It soon becomes crystal clear that the thief will not hesitate to kill anyone who gets in his way as the story races to a dramatic ending.

The Keeper (DI Redding Book 2)

When the body of a young Helensburgh woman is washed up on the shore of the River Clyde, DI Claire Redding takes on what turns out to be the biggest case of her career to date.

The mystery deepens when forensic evidence found on the body reveals surprising results. However, pressure builds on Claire when the body of a well-known local man is washed up a few days later and the young detective has not only to overcome some very serious personal issues but must solve the case quickly.

Full of drama and mystery, this page turner will keep you on the edge of your seat until the very last page.

Who put that Spaceship on my school!?

(Illustrated by Elle Hunter)

This wonderful children's bedtime story is about a young boy - Jack, who makes friends with a small alien called Bizak after he accidentally lands his spaceship on top of Jack's primary school in Dumbarton. Much to Jack's surprise Bizak asks for help and together they fly off into outer space on the adventure of a lifetime.

Printed in Great Britain
by Amazon